The security guard's
arm. 'Come on. Fun's

Outside, Mitch sat
closed his eyes, trying to conjure up the face he'd seen,
in the sketch. Was he right?

Yes, definitely. He was as certain as he could be.

The man they suspected of walking out with a five million dollar painting under his arm was the man who had come into Cyber-Snax earlier that week. Mitch had helped him send the message over the Net to the trans-Atlantic yacht race bulletin board …

Titles in the

INTERNET DETECTIVES

series

1. NET BANDITS
2. ESCAPE KEY
3. SPEED SURF
4. CYBER FEUD
5. SYSTEM CRASH
6. WEB TRAP
7. VIRUS ATTACK
8. ACCESS DENIED

INTERNET DETECTIVES

A WORKING PARTNERS BOOK

MACMILLAN CHILDREN'S BOOKS

First published 1996 by Macmillan Children's Books
a division of Macmillan Publishers Limited
25 Eccleston Place, London SW1W 9NF
and Basingstoke

Associated companies throughout the world

Created by Working Partners Limited
London W6 0HE

ISBN 0 330 34736 5

Computer graphics by Jason Levy

9 8 7 6 5 4

A CIP catalogue record for this book is available from
the British Library.

Printed by Mackays of Chatham plc, Kent

speed surf

The white-topped waves loomed high above Josh's head. It was all he could do to stop himself crying out in fear.

As the water crashed down, he turned his head away. Into his ears hammered the sounds of a wave pounding onto the yacht's foredeck and fierce hissing as the water sluiced over the side and back into the sea.

Breathing heavily, he looked up. The yacht's sails, large and fat-bellied, were filled with the wind he could hear howling around him. At his side, almost within touching distance, the sea was rushing past.

Another wave crashed against the bow, then another, sending spray high into the air. Josh could almost taste the salt on his lips.

He peered ahead. The horizon was barely visible, merging with the grey clouds. Looking this way and that, there was no sign of land. He was alone, totally alone, in the middle of the Atlantic Ocean.

And then everything went dark.

Portsmouth, England.
Sunday 2nd June, 2.40 p.m.

Taking off the Virtual Reality headset, Josh Allan took a couple of seconds to adjust to the fact that he wasn't alone on a racing yacht but in a bedroom with his two friends, Tamsyn Smith and Rob Zanelli. He'd been watching a VR program using Rob's computer.

'That was *excellent,*' said Josh. It was just like being there!'

Rob grinned. 'Yeah, but wouldn't you like to be there for *real,* Josh? Sailing across the Atlantic on your own?'

Josh shook his head, a shock of brown hair flying in all directions. 'No way! A VR program is as close as I want to get to the ocean.'

Tamsyn laughed. 'For once, I agree with Josh one hundred per cent! I like to feel the dry land under my feet.'

'Well, I'd love it,' Rob said. He leaned forward to slip the sailing program CD-ROM from his computer.

'Did you say there was more on that?' Tamsyn asked, pointing to the disk in Rob's hand.

'Yeah, a sort of guided tour of below deck at the start. It's amazing how much you can't see from the outside. Those boats have everything, y'know.'

Tamsyn reached for the VR headset.'Can I try it?'

Rob shook his head. 'Not right now, I want to log into the Net. I'm expecting some sea-mail!'

As he quit the VR program, Rob's screen

changed to show its home page. He double-clicked the mouse on a globe icon.

'I know I shouldn't ask,' sighed Josh, 'but why did you say "sea-mail" instead of "e-mail"?'

Rob's grin grew wider. 'Josh, my man,' he said, 'You're just gonna have to wait and *see* ...'

They didn't have long to wait. Moments later, the screen display changed. Rob's computer was now connected to the world-wide network of computers known as the Internet. Up on the screen flashed a start menu of choices.

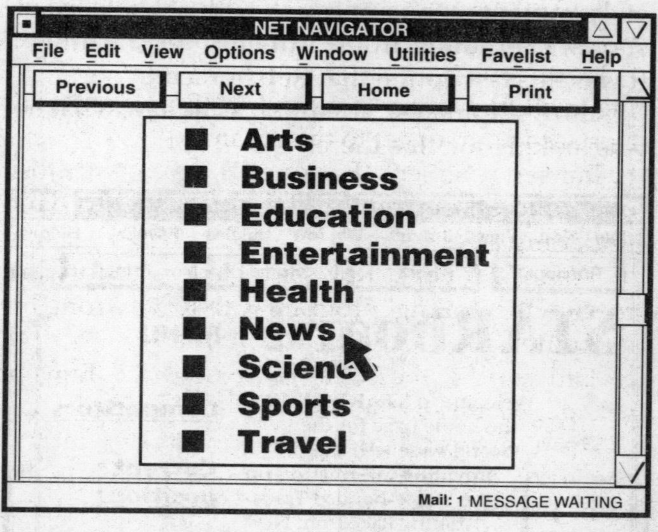

Rob had been an Internet user for some time. After the car accident which had confined Rob to a wheelchair, his parents hadn't been prepared to send him to an ordinary school. For a long time he'd been taught at home, and his only way of making friends had been over the Net.

That was how he'd first got in touch with Tamsyn and Josh, after their school joined the Internet. Now that Rob went to Abbey School as well, they met every day for real.

'One waiting,' said Josh, pointing at the message on the bottom line. 'Is that it?'

'No, that's e-mail,' said Rob. 'Sea-mail is somewhere else!'

He moved the mouse cursor across the screen and clicked on the item marked 'Sport'. Immediately another menu appeared, with a whole list of sports, everything from 'Athletics' to 'Yachting'. It was this last option that Rob homed in on.

'Ahoy, shipmates!' cried Rob as he saw what he was looking for. 'It's there!'

He motioned to Tamsyn to take over the mouse. 'Try clicking on Competitors,' he said.

A list of names flashed up: the yachts taking part in the race, their sponsors, and the yachtsmen and women who would be sailing them.

'Either of you see a name you recognize?' said Rob, looking from Tamsyn to Josh.

They both scanned the list – and saw, in the middle, what Rob was getting at.

GO GAMEZONE (Brad Stewart.
Sponsor: GAMEZONE LTD)

'*GAMEZONE*?' said Tamsyn, wide-eyed. *GAMEZONE* was the name of the computer games company owned by Rob's parents. 'You mean your parents are sponsoring a yacht in a big race? I'm impressed!'

Rob nodded, clearly delighted. He picked up the shiny CD-ROM. 'Not any old yacht, Tamsyn. The yacht on here. The one you've just been sailing, Josh!'

'Yeah? Cool.'

'And you've been keeping it to yourself?' said Tamsyn.

'Not quite,' said Rob, teasingly. 'I've already fired off notes to the others to tell them about it.'

He meant Tom, Lauren and Mitch, three friends they'd all made over the Internet. Tom lived in Australia, Lauren in Canada and Mitch in America.

'But you didn't tell us!' cried Tamsyn.

Rob held up his hands. 'Hey, I wanted to tell you two personally! Besides, I only found out myself a couple of days ago. I couldn't believe it when Mum and Dad told me.'

'That they'd bought that boat, you mean?' said Josh. 'I'd have had trouble believing that as well.'

'They haven't bought it. They're just sponsoring it – putting up some money to help with the costs, in return for having the company's name on the yacht.'

'Why?' asked Josh.

Tamsyn tapped at the computer screen. 'Advertising. If the race details are on the Net ...'

'And on TV,' added Rob, 'and splashed all over the papers ...'

'Then the whole world will have heard of *GAMEZONE* by the time the race is finished. Especially if *GO GAMEZONE* wins!'

'Or sinks!' said Josh making wild rolling motions in his chair.

'Josh!' Tamsyn hurled a cushion in his direction.

'Don't worry, Tamsyn,' said Rob. 'If Brad Stewart's as good a yachtsman as Dad says, then there's no chance of that happening. He might not win, but he definitely won't sink!'

'He's going to be sailing on his *own*?' Tamsyn asked.

Rob nodded. 'Scary, huh? He's done loads of single-handed racing before, though. He shot the video for that CD-ROM during his last trip. It certainly got Mum and Dad interested.

Apparently they've been thinking of expanding into VR games, and the minute they saw Brad's video they realized just how good a sailing one would be. Bingo – they turn it into a demo CD-ROM.'

'Now I understand why you were going on about sea-mail!' said Josh.

'Ah, not completely,' said Rob. He clicked on the MAIL WAITING part of the status line. At once the screen display changed to show the list of electronic mail items that Rob hadn't yet filed. He selected the new arrival, at the top of the list.

```
From: BRAD@STAR.COM
To: ZMASTER@PRIME.CO.UK
```

Josh looked at who the note was from. 'Brad? Not *the* Brad?'

'Sure is. The company who've set up the STARBOARD Internet web site are organizing the whole event as a clever way of showing what can be done with communications equipment nowadays.'

'Not *their* communications equipment, by any chance?' Tamsyn asked.

'Of course,' said Rob. 'What's more, they've supplied all the yachts with it – portable PCs, radio modems, the lot. They'll be using it to get weather reports from the Net, that sort of thing.'

Josh pointed at the message on screen. 'Don't tell me. You thought you'd give the system a test and send Brad Stewart a note.'

Rob laughed. 'Got it in one, my boy!'

They read the reply from Brad Stewart, each trying to picture the yachtsman sitting at his portable PC on board *GO GAMEZONE*

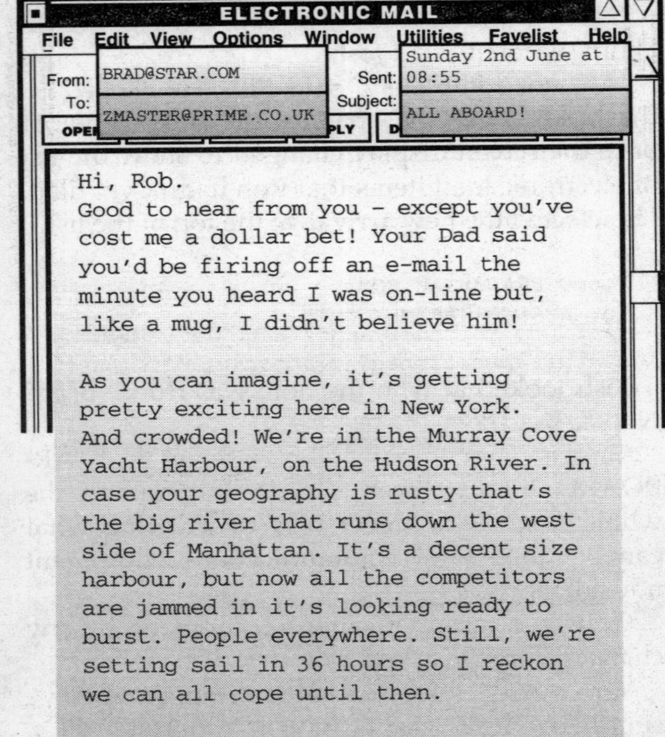

ELECTRONIC MAIL

File Edit View Options Window Utilities Favelist Help

From: BRAD@STAR.COM
To: ZMASTER@PRIME.CO.UK
Sent: Sunday 2nd June at 08:55
Subject: ALL ABOARD!

Hi, Rob.
Good to hear from you - except you've cost me a dollar bet! Your Dad said you'd be firing off an e-mail the minute you heard I was on-line but, like a mug, I didn't believe him!

As you can imagine, it's getting pretty exciting here in New York. And crowded! We're in the Murray Cove Yacht Harbour, on the Hudson River. In case your geography is rusty that's the big river that runs down the west side of Manhattan. It's a decent size harbour, but now all the competitors are jammed in it's looking ready to burst. People everywhere. Still, we're setting sail in 36 hours so I reckon we can all cope until then.

I'm pretty well prepared for the trip. If the weather people are right, and we get the good westerly winds they're forecasting, I could make the crossing in about 17 days.

'By ... the 20th of June?' said Tamsyn.
'Just after our exams finish,' said Rob.
Josh groaned loudly. 'Don't talk about exams. Don't even mention exams.'

```
It's getting a bit tense here,
too. None of us wants anything to
go wrong, of course. The race is
getting a mountain of publicity
and the harbour's been buzzing
with sightseers. Nobody minds
them, just so long as they don't
turn into souvenir-hunters and
start lifting things. That's why
most of the yachts have intruder
alarms fitted nowadays.

Mind you, even they can be a
pain. GO GAMEZONE's alarm went
off last night, and I had to be
dragged from my bed to shut it
up!
```

'Alarm?' said Josh at once.
They looked at one another. Solving intriguing puzzles over the Internet was something they were becoming very good at.
'Read the next bit,' said Tamsyn, looking back at the screen.

As you might have worked out, I wasn't on board. We're a superstitious lot, us sailors, and one of my superstitions is to sleep in a soft hotel bed for a couple nights before setting sail – the theory being that it'll bring me a smooth crossing. There's method in my madness, mind: whether it does or not, at least I get some decent shut-eye, which is what I *won't* get for the next 17 days!
Anyhow, it must have been a false alarm. Nothing was missing. Even so, I'll be giving this particular superstition a miss tonight and sleeping on board just in case.

'Sorted, then,' said Josh, sounding disappointed.

'Pity,' said Rob. As he hit PAGE DOWN to scroll to the remainder of Brad's note, his eyes brightened. 'Still, there's no reason why Mitch can't check it out while he's there ...'

And, sure, I'd love to show your pal Mitch over GO GAMEZONE. Tell him to head for Berth 42 – and it'll have to be before noon

```
tomorrow. The race starts at 3pm
our time, and I'll need some final
prep. time.
OK, Rob, that's all. Next time you
hear from me I'll be on the
Atlantic Ocean somewhere!

Brad
```

Mail:

'Mitch is going to see the yacht?' said Tamsyn.

'Looks like it!' said Rob. 'Before I e-mailed Brad, I sent a note to Mitch telling him about the race and everything. He fired me back a reply so fast it was hot!'

'Asking if he could have a look over *GO GAMEZONE*?'

'Right,' said Rob. 'He said he'd always wanted to see a racing yacht close up, ever since he sailed models on the lake in Central Park as a kid! So when I contacted Brad, I asked. Mitch is gonna owe me something wicked when he sees this!'

Mitch Zanelli lived in New York. He was one of the first friends Rob had made over the Internet, after Rob had contacted him to see if they were related. They had stayed in touch ever since. Together with Lauren and Tom, and his two friends from Abbey School, they'd used the Internet to solve more than one mystery.

Moving the mouse cursor across the screen,

Rob clicked on the FORWARD button. Moments later he was tacking a short note onto the front of Brad's.

Tamsyn and Josh leaned forward, one on either side of Rob. 'Don't forget to mention the alarm,' said Tamsyn.

Rob grinned. 'I wasn't going to.'

CHAPTER 2

New York, USA.
Monday 3rd June, 9.05 a.m.

Mitch looked anxiously at his watch. It was going to take him at least an hour on the subway to get to Murray Cove Yacht Harbour. The place was right down in the southern tip of Manhattan.

He looked out of the window yet again. So where was Mr Lewin?

Mr Lewin was Mitch's boss. While studying at college, Mitch was working part-time in a café called Cyber-Snax, near New York's Central Park. It was a special kind of café, one that had Internet computers so that customers could sip their coffee and surf the Net at the same time.

Working there was great as far as Mitch was concerned – not only did he get paid, but when his work was done he had the perk of free air-time on the Net as well.

The difference was that, *this* morning, he didn't want to log in ... he wanted to go out!

When Mitch had told Mr Lewin about

Brad Stewart's offer, his boss had been happy to rearrange his work hours.

'Sure,' he'd said. 'Monday mornings are always quiet. You can shoot off the minute I get back from my jog.'

That was the problem. Mr Lewin's early-morning jog in Central Park usually meant that he'd run *to* somewhere and then walk back. But this morning, thought Mitch, his boss had obviously managed to run further than usual.

Mitch took another look out of the window. Still no sign. He was going to have to dash the instant Mr Lewin showed. He went out to the small back room to collect his things together. Mitch was studying photography and this would be a perfect chance to add to his portfolio of sailing shots. He tucked his camera and a notebook into his rucksack.

The harsh sound of the door buzzer told him that somebody had come into the café. Grabbing his gear, Mitch dived out – only to see at once that it wasn't Mr Lewin, but the café's first customer of the day. Standing on the other side of the counter was a slim, wiry-looking man dressed in jeans and a denim jacket. He had a narrow face, and his hair was slicked back.

'You know how to use these, kid?' the man said, jerking a thumb towards the row of PCs.

'Sure,' said Mitch. 'You want coffee?'

The man shook his head sharply. 'Nothing. I

got a message to send. All I want is for you to show me how.'

Mitch nodded. 'No problem.' He stepped over to one of the PCs. 'You know anything about using the Net?' he asked.

'No,' snapped the man. 'And I don't want to. I just want this job done, and the quicker the better. So you just sit down, huh?'

Mitch did as he was told, remembering what Mr Lewin had told him on his first day: *The customer is always right, Mitch – even if he is a jug-head.*

The man dipped into a pocket and pulled out a slip of paper.

'OK. I got to send a message to a web site. That make sense to you?'

'Sure,' said Mitch. 'Which one?'

The man consulted his slip of paper again. 'STARBOARD.' He spelled it out, letter by letter.

'The web site for the single-handed yacht race,' said Mitch. 'Is that the one you mean?'

Standing over him, the man looked irritated. He paused, then thrust the slip of paper towards Mitch. 'Just do what it says.'

Mitch glanced at it. The instructions were written in bold, capital letters. Quickly, Mitch accessed the STARBOARD home page, then clicked on the underlined word 'Messages'. A simple form box came up.

NET NAVIGATOR

File Edit View Options Window Utilities Favelist Help

Previous Next Home Print

STARboard
MESSAGES

Send your message to the competitors in the STAR Single-handed Trans-Atlantic Race!

To:

Message:

From:

Mail:

Mitch looked at the message on the slip. 'This all? No names?'

'No names,' snapped the man. 'Come on, kid, cut the questions. Just get on with it.'

The message was short. Positioning the cursor on the form, Mitch typed.

```
GOOD SPEED ABOARD CROSSING THE DEEP.
BACK SAFE
```

'All done,' said Mitch.

The man let out a sigh, as if he was relieved. 'How long will that take to get there?'

Mitch looked up. *Doesn't this guy know ANYTHING?* Quickly entering the STARBOARD message area, he displayed the results of his handiwork.

'It's *already* there,' said Mitch, showing the man his own message. 'You see? If we can read it, anybody who connects to this web site will be able to read it as well.'

'Good, good.' The man produced a ten-dollar bill and thrust it into Mitch's hand. 'Thanks, kid.'

He was out of the door almost before Mitch could say thanks back and, by the time Mr Lewin came puffing across the street moments later, was long gone.

Murray Cove Yacht Harbour, New York. 10.32 a.m.

Mitch raced down Vesey Street, and into Murray Avenue. Towering above him to his left were the massive twin skyscrapers of the World Trade Centre, over 400 metres high and the tallest buildings in New York City.

Mitch didn't notice them. He had eyes only for what he could see ahead of him – the forest of masts belonging to the yachts berthed in the Murray Cove Yacht Harbour. Which one belonged to *GO GAMEZONE*, he wondered.

There were crowds milling around the entrance to the harbour, some going in and some coming out. Like Mitch, many of the spectators had cameras slung round their necks. Pushing his way through, Mitch looked around.

The sight was amazing. The whole harbour

was jammed with rows of glistening white yachts, their masts stretching tall against the blue sky. The air was filled with the sounds of halyards – the ropes used to raise the sails – pinging against their masts.

He headed round the harbour edge, looking for Berth 42. It was in the far corner of the square harbour. As he walked further from the entrance the crowds thinned considerably.

38, 39, Berth 40, Berth 41.

Mitch stopped to stare at the yacht in Berth 41. With the name *JIMMY THE ONE* emblazoned in crimson on its side, the boat looked brilliant. Lifting his camera Mitch focussed on it, then put it down again as a man came up on deck.

The man had closely-shaven hair, and was powerfully built. He paused to look at Mitch, then set about tidying some tarpaulins. But, as he moved on, Mitch knew he was being watched.

In Berth 42 *GO GAMEZONE* sat high in the water, its gangplank angled down to the harbour side. It was smaller than *JIMMY THE ONE,* but Mitch still thought it looked great. Focusing his camera, he took a couple of shots.

He looked around but there was no sign of anybody. He didn't know what Brad Stewart looked like and wondered what he should do now. Mitch made a move towards the gangplank.

'Hey, you!' yelled an angry voice. 'Where do you think you're going?'

Mitch stepped back as he saw the man on the

deck of *JIMMY THE ONE* leap down onto the harbourside.

'Cool it,' said Mitch as the man raced up to him. 'I'm here to see Brad Stewart.'

'Oh, yeah?' snapped Shaven-head. 'What's your name?'

'Mitch Zanelli?' At the sound of another voice, Mitch swung round to see a face pop up from *GO GAMEZONE*'s cockpit.

'That's me,' said a relieved Mitch. 'You Brad?'

The face broke into a smile. 'Yeah. Come aboard.'

Next to Mitch, Shaven-head scowled as Brad Stewart called over, 'It's OK, Jim. I'm expecting him. But thanks anyway.'

'What did he think I was going to do?' said Mitch as he clambered up the gangplank. 'Sail off into the sunset?'

Brad Stewart laughed. He had a sun-tanned face which looked as though it spent most of its time outdoors. 'You don't look like a sailor to me, Mitch.'

Mitch looked out to where Shaven-head was stomping back to *JIMMY THE ONE*. 'Well *he* doesn't look like a sailor to *me*! Who is he, anyway?'

'Jim Gilroy,' said Brad. 'And don't go on looks, Mitch. He'll get to Portsmouth before I do.'

'Yeah? He's good then?'

'He's got a bigger *and* faster yacht. But we're in different classes of the race, so we're not really rivals.' He grinned. 'Maybe if we were, then he'd have left you alone in the hope that you *were* going to pinch *GO GAMEZONE*!'

'The only thing I'm planning to take is photographs,' said Mitch.

Brad Stewart took him over every part of *GO GAMEZONE*, from bow to stern on the sleek yacht's deck, to the tiny galley and sleeping berths below. Mitch clicked away at each and every stop.

'Hey, is there anything this boat hasn't got?' said Mitch as he was shown into what looked like a small living room. It had bench seats round the sides and a table in the middle. There were even pictures on the walls.

'No,' said the yachtsman. 'Not that I'll be getting much saloon-time on the way over.'

'Saloon? Like in cowboy movies?'

Brad waved an arm. 'This is called the saloon. When there's a full crew, those not on duty relax in here. On my own, I won't get to see it!'

Mitch took some more photographs, then followed Brad out as he was led back to *GO GAMEZONE*'s cockpit with its impressive navigational instruments.

'I take it there's no way water can get in here?' asked Mitch. 'I mean, electronics and water don't mix so well – and you *are* gonna be in the middle of the ocean!'

'Good point,' said Brad. He pointed up at the solid perspex enclosing the cockpit. 'This is a pretty watertight area, though. And most of the equipment has got its own protection.'

He pointed at the portable PC at the side of the cockpit. 'Except for that, of course,' he added. 'Putting that on board was a last-minute decision by the race organizers. How it'll stand up to three weeks bouncing around in a damp atmosphere I don't know. But ... no computer, no Internet.'

As the Net was mentioned, Mitch remembered what Rob had asked him to check out. He pointed at the cockpit console.

'This control the alarm system, too?'

'Alarm?' Brad Stewart raised an eyebrow.

'Rob said *GO GAMEZONE*'s alarm went off the other night. I was just wondering if it was controlled from in here too.'

'Nothing so sophisticated, Mitch,' said Brad. He bent down and lifted the rubber mat at the opening to the cockpit. Beneath, there was a small oblong of plastic, with wires leading from it. 'Just a simple pressure pad system. There's a few of these pads dotted around the yacht. The alarm sounds if any one of them is stepped on.'

Mitch nodded towards the yacht in the next berth. 'With Grim Jim on the lookout, I'm amazed anyone got *far enough* to step on it.'

Brad laughed. 'Oh, Bruno could get past anyone!'

'Bruno?' said Mitch. 'You know who it was?'

'Pretty sure, yes,' said Brad.

'You call the cops?'

Brad shook his head. 'No point. Bruno's a dog.'

He pointed back along the quay. A large, brown mongrel dog was snuffling around a stack of cardboard boxes and empty oil drums. 'He thinks he owns the place,' Brad went on, 'always running up and down gangplanks. Don't know why I didn't think of him before.'

'You reckon *he* stepped on your alarm?' said Mitch.

'Trampled, more like,' said Brad as they watched Bruno dive into the boxes and out again. 'Jim Gilroy suggested he might have been the culprit, and I'm inclined to agree!'

No mystery then, thought Mitch as he strolled back along the quay after saying his thanks and leaving Brad Stewart to his final preparations. He sat down on a bench near the cardboard boxes. The brown mongrel had disappeared.

Mitch took more photographs as the yachts began to leave the harbour. *JIMMY THE ONE*'s engine eventually started up with a roar, the shaven-headed Jim Gilroy easing his beautiful yacht away from the quayside to begin the journey down the Hudson River, past the Statue of Liberty and on to the start point off Staten Island.

Only as Brad Stewart started *GO GAMEZONE* on its way out of the harbour with a cheery thumbs-up did Mitch think of leaving. He checked his camera. The picture count was on thirty-five; only one shot left on his last thirty-six print roll of film.

Just then, he heard a scrabbling sound coming from nearby. The large brown dog hadn't left the cardboard boxes; he'd settled down in the middle of them for a snooze. Now he was awake and attacking them again.

'Hey, Bruno,' called Mitch as the dog pulled one of the boxes over onto its side and began pawing at something inside it. 'What you doing, boy?'

Laughing, Mitch took the final shot from his roll of film of Bruno with his head almost completely inside the box. The dog had found something wrapped in newspaper. As Mitch approached, Bruno scampered off.

'No good to eat, huh?' Mitch called after him.

He kicked at some rubbish in an attempt to clear up the mess – and saw what Bruno had found. Wrapped in some pages of the *New York Times* was a very small painting in a gilded frame. 'Definitely no good to eat!' said Mitch.

And somebody reckons it's no good to hang up, either, he thought. The painting had obviously been dumped in the box for the garbage collectors to take, along with all the other boxes left behind after the yachts had been stocked with provisions for their three-week voyages.

It showed a galleon in full sail, fighting its way through white-flecked waves. Although no bigger than a magazine in size, the detail was wonderful. *Well, I like it,* thought Mitch. A pint-sized painting would suit the pint-sized room he had to study in!

Wrapping it up again, Mitch tucked the painting into his rucksack. Two hours later, as a gun cracked to send GO GAMEZONE and the other racing yachts off on their journey across the Atlantic, Mitch was hanging the painting on his wall.

CHAPTER 3

Abbey School.
Tuesday 4th June, 8.40 a.m.

'I hate exams,' groaned Josh.

Tamsyn pushed her bike into a rack and shackled it securely. 'Come on, Josh. They don't start until next week. It's revising that's the killer.'

Josh locked his bike up. 'I hate revising as well!' he said. 'You spend ages boning up on stuff, just so you can write it down as fast as you can and then forget about it all over again.'

Tamsyn laughed. 'I think the idea is that you *don't* forget it all again.'

The two friends started walking towards the school buildings. 'Say what you like,' said Josh, 'exams and revision just get in the way of the important things in life.'

'Such as?' said Tamsyn.

'Such as football. And music. And food … and Net surfing!' shouted Josh, breaking into a sprint. 'Come on, there's Rob!'

They caught up with Rob as he was pushing himself along the main corridor of the Technology Block. Josh grabbed the handles of Rob's wheelchair and gave it a quick shove. 'And it's the Zanelli Zipper, forging ahead in the Abbey School Trans-Technology Block race …'

'You'll have to push harder than that, Josh! I'll never get there!'

Still laughing, they piled into a room marked COMPUTER CLUB. In it were a number of PCs, all connected to the Internet. Rob quickly logged into one. There were three e-mails waiting for him.

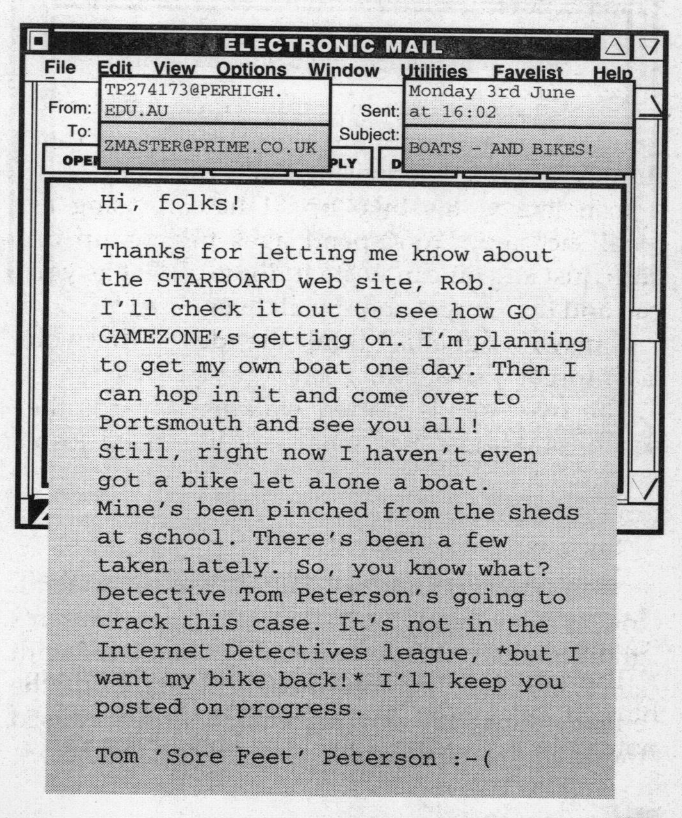

Hi, folks!

Thanks for letting me know about the STARBOARD web site, Rob. I'll check it out to see how GO GAMEZONE's getting on. I'm planning to get my own boat one day. Then I can hop in it and come over to Portsmouth and see you all! Still, right now I haven't even got a bike let alone a boat. Mine's been pinched from the sheds at school. There's been a few taken lately. So, you know what? Detective Tom Peterson's going to crack this case. It's not in the Internet Detectives league, *but I want my bike back!* I'll keep you posted on progress.

Tom 'Sore Feet' Peterson :-(

Tamsyn whistled. 'I pity whoever's responsible. With Tom on their trail they've got no chance!'

Rob closed the note, then opened the next. It was from Lauren.

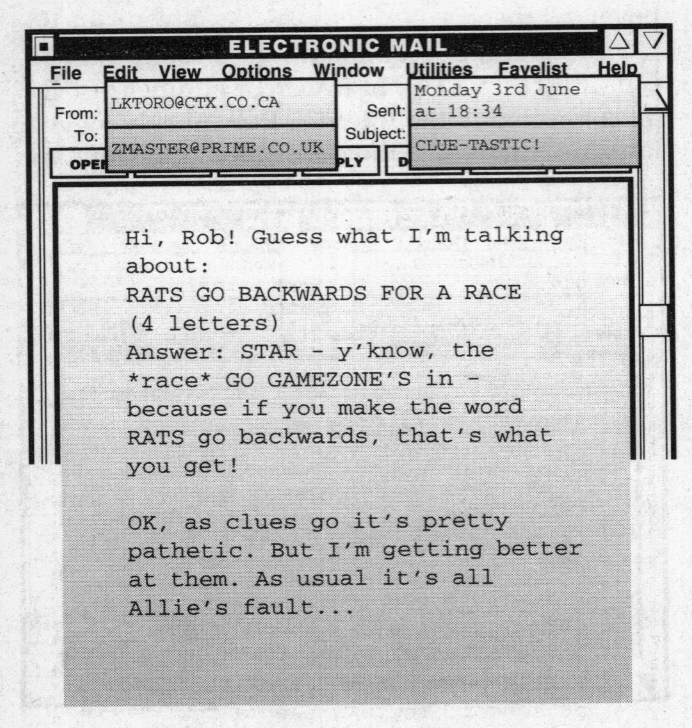
ELECTRONIC MAIL

File Edit View Options Window Utilities Favelist Help

From: LKTORO@CTX.CO.CA
To: ZMASTER@PRIME.CO.UK
Sent: Monday 3rd June at 18:34
Subject: CLUE-TASTIC!

Hi, Rob! Guess what I'm talking about:
RATS GO BACKWARDS FOR A RACE (4 letters)
Answer: STAR - y'know, the *race* GO GAMEZONE'S in - because if you make the word RATS go backwards, that's what you get!

OK, as clues go it's pretty pathetic. But I'm getting better at them. As usual it's all Allie's fault...

Rob, Tamsyn and Josh found themselves smiling as they read the note. Allie was Lauren's grandmother, Alice, whom Lauren had lived with since her own parents died. Judging from the e-mails they both sent out, which of them caused the other the most trouble was difficult to say!

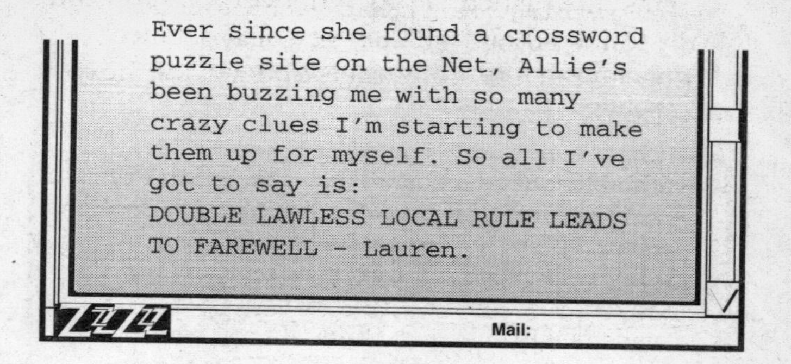
Ever since she found a crossword puzzle site on the Net, Allie's been buzzing me with so many crazy clues I'm starting to make them up for myself. So all I've got to say is:
DOUBLE LAWLESS LOCAL RULE LEADS TO FAREWELL - Lauren.

'Huh?' frowned Josh.

'C'mon, Josh,' said Rob, 'get that brain in gear. A local rule is a "bye-law", so a law*less* local rule is a "bye" ...'

Tamsyn had seen it, too. 'And a double "bye" equals "bye-bye" – get it?'

'I get it,' groaned Josh. 'Very clever! Not.'

Rob clicked on the OPEN button to read the third e-mail. 'This'll be a good one, people,' he said.

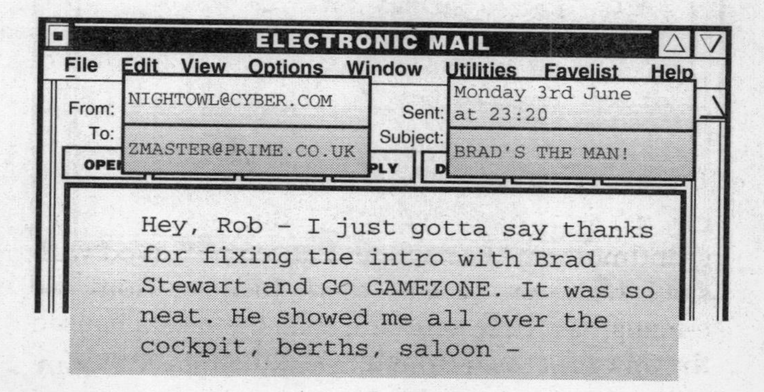

Hey, Rob - I just gotta say thanks for fixing the intro with Brad Stewart and GO GAMEZONE. It was so neat. He showed me all over the cockpit, berths, saloon -

everything. Man, that yacht's better than a house. It wouldn't have surprised me if somebody *had* wanted to steal it!

That's not why the alarm went off, though. Brad reckons it was probably set off by a loopy dog called Bruno that seems to have the run of the yacht harbour. I agree with him. Anybody else would have had to get past a skinhead called Gilroy who was on the next-door yacht. The guy was ready to clap me in irons till Brad told him I was on the level.

So, mystery solved - Bruno's the villain. Mind you, I'm not going to turn in the mutt. He led me to find a real groovy painting of an old ship somebody had thrown out. It's only tiny but it's got incredible detail.

I'll be checking the Net for race news real regular from now on. Hey - check out the on-line NYT sports pages. There's some great pictures of the start. Wish I could take 'em like that!

Anyways, gotta split. This night-owl's bushed!

Mitch

ZZZZ Mail:

'NYT?' said Tamsyn.

'The *New York Times,*' Rob said. 'We can

look at it on the Net.'

The rasp of the school bell interrupted them. 'Not now we can't,' said Josh, getting to his feet. 'Ms Gillies awaits.'

Rob looked reluctant to move. 'Hey, I'd really like to check out that newspaper.'

Tamsyn tut-tutted. 'Ms Gillies said she was going to revise the *whole* of *Oliver Twist* this morning, and you know how keen you guys are on revision.' She took the mouse from Rob and clicked on QUIT. 'So, let's go. The NYT will have to wait!'

Perth, Australia.
Tuesday 4th June, 5 p.m. (UK time 9 a.m.)

Tom Peterson angrily kicked open the garden gate and stomped up the garden path. An hour late home!

Letting himself in, he threw his rucksack down on the sofa and flopped down beside it. An hour! That wasn't a problem when he *wanted* to be late, but when he wanted to be home early …

'Miss the bus?' said Mrs Peterson, looking in.

Tom nodded. Bus or bike, he could be home in twenty minutes. But missing the bus *and* having had your bike stolen – bad news.

What he couldn't understand was how the thief could get away with it. The bike racks were in the open, visible from all parts of the school. How could somebody just walk in to the school unnoticed – on a Friday of all days, when most of the kids were gazing out of the window dreaming of the weekend?

On a Friday ...

Tom leapt up and grabbed the calendar sitting on the sideboard. Debbie Levitt's bike had vanished on May 3rd, Kerry Archer's on May 17th. Both Fridays, two weeks apart. And his own had been stolen on Friday 31st – another two weeks!

It was a definite pattern. Tom's dad was a detective in the Perth police, and he was always talking about looking for patterns in crimes. Might whoever-it-was be targeting their school on Fridays, and every other week? Because if so, that would make the next date ... Tom checked the calendar ... Friday, 14th June. Almost two weeks away.

He sat back, a determined look on his face. By then, he was going to have a plan ready.

Abbey School. Tuesday 4th June, 12.20 p.m.

Rob settled himself in front of the keyboard with a sigh of pleasure. He'd been looking forward to this moment all morning.

After logging in to the Internet, reaching the on-line version of the the *New York Times* took seconds. Starting at the home menu he selected 'NEWS'. This brought up another menu which had INTERNATIONAL, NATIONAL and LOCAL in it. Rob clicked on INTERNATIONAL. He was presented with a list from which he could choose to look at newspapers from all over the world. The entry reading *New York Times* was halfway down the list.

'So, which one's *GO GAMEZONE*?' said Josh, peering over Rob's shoulder as he found the photograph Mitch had mentioned. Tamsyn craned over them both to catch a look too. It was a long-distance shot showing a host of yachts milling about at the start of the race, their sails billowing in the wind.

Rob shook his head. 'Don't ask me. But it must be there somewhere.'

'Isn't there a report?' asked Tamsyn.

Rob scrolled the page back and forth. The photograph had no more than a caption, and a very short report next to it. Beneath that, a note indicated: 'Full Report, Page 41'.

'Wind through to page 41, skipper!' said Josh. 'Page down until you get there!'

'Page down, simple seaman?' said Rob. 'This skipper lets the system do the work!'

At the bottom of the screen was a button marked SEARCH. Rob clicked on it. Immediately a panel popped up:

SEARCH FOR?

Rob simply typed: SAIL.

'There could be more than one report on it,' he said as he hit the Return key. 'This way we get the lot.'

'Give that man a medal,' said Tamsyn as, moments later, the results of the search flashed up on the screen. '*Two* reports to do with sailing.'

```
Search Results

Found 2 matches containing sail.

1. STAR begins: Transatlantic sailors on
their way.
2. 'In Full Sail' Stolen. Valuable
painting goes missing.
```

As they stared at the second item their search had turned up, looking for the race report took a back seat.

'Painting?' said Rob.

'Not the one Mitch found, surely?' began Tamsyn. 'No, it couldn't ...'

Rob clicked on the second line. After a short pause, the section from the the *New York Times* flashed up in front of them.

'IN FULL SAIL' STOLEN

Valuable Painting Goes Missing

A masterpiece by the classic English painter William Turner has been stolen from the Manhattan Gallery in an audacious robbery.

The painting, a water-colour, is called 'In Full Sail' and shows a man-of-war galleon on the high seas. Dating from 1826, it was on loan from the Clore Gallery for the Turner Collection in London. It is estimated to be worth well over $5 million.

Josh whistled. 'Five million dollars! What's that in real money?'

'A lot! Over three million pounds,' said Tamsyn. She shook her head in amazement. 'How can a picture be worth that much?'

'Especially one as small as that,' said Rob. He was pointing at the next part of the newspaper article.

The picture is a miniature, measuring 16cm x 24cm. It was because of its size that the thief was able to steal it the way he did, hidden in a newspaper he was carrying.

Detective Chuck Matthews of the New York Police Department, in charge of the investigation, said: 'The security video clearly shows a man snatching the picture from the wall, then folding it into a newspaper before running out through a fire escape door.' The thief had clearly done his homework. All the normal exits had been covered by guards but – in what is seen as an embarrassing security oversight by the gallery director, Ms Caroline O'Connell – the emergency exits were unguarded.

The robbery took place at 5.40pm on Friday evening, May 31st, just before the Manhattan Gallery closed. Defending her decision not to release the news until now, Ms O'Connell said: 'I thought that if the thief was an opportunist who didn't know how much the painting was worth, and he then heard about it on the news, he might take fright and destroy it rather than risk being caught with it in his possession.'

Detective Matthews now believes the thief knew exactly what he was after. 'It could have been stolen to order, maybe for a private collection overseas. We're putting an extra watch on airports and ports, but there must be a chance that the painting is already out of the country.'

Mail:

'Do you really think the painting Mitch found could be the stolen one?' said Tamsyn.

'It sounds pretty much like it, doesn't it?' said Rob. 'He said it was a seascape ...'

'A tiny one,' Josh cut in, 'with a lot of detail.' He aimed a finger at the screen. 'And has that got a lot of detail, or what?'

At the side of the report was a photograph of the painting. With its view of old harbour buildings and the fighting ship in full sail it was difficult to believe the actual painting was no bigger than the size of a magazine.

'Well, there's only one way to find out,' said Rob. 'And I'll fill in the others while I'm at it.'

Quitting the Net Navigator, he went into e-mail and retrieved Mitch's earlier note. He clicked on the REPLY button:

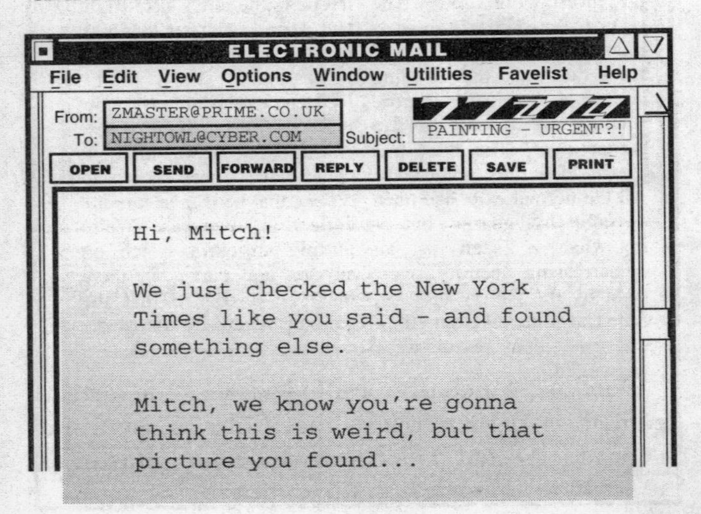

CHAPTER 4

Cyber-Snax Café, New York.
Thursday 6th June, midnight.

```
... sounds like it could be a
painting that was nicked from
the Manhattan Gallery last
Friday. Is that anywhere near
where you found the picture?
Hey, and if it *is* the one,
don't forget we told you about
it first. There could be a
reward y'know - that picture's
supposed to be worth $5 million!
```

Mail:

Mitch stared at the note he'd just seen. Sent two days ago! He'd been so busy he'd not had time to log in.

Quickly, Mitch too pulled down the article from the *New York Times* that Rob, Tamsyn and Josh had spotted. His heart was beating faster as he scrolled through it, until ...

There it was – *his* painting! The one he'd saved from being mauled by Bruno the brute. The one he'd hung on his wall. The *stolen* painting!

Mitch ran all the way back to the dingy tenement block he called home. Racing up to the cramped third-floor apartment he lived in with his parents, two younger brothers and baby sister, his thoughts were moving as fast as his feet.

A five million dollar picture. There had to be a reward. A *big* reward!

Mitch let himself in. Everybody else was asleep. Being careful not to make a sound, Mitch crept into the tiny boxroom that was his own. It had enough room for a bed and a chair, no more. His clothes were hanging from hooks along the wall.

And there, between his shirt and jeans, was the painting.

Lifting it down, Mitch looked at it again. Was it really the one?

He had a sudden thought. Putting the painting on his bed, he dived for the wastebin. The copy of the *New York Times* it had been wrapped in ...

It was still there! Mitch yanked the paper out of the bin. The date at the top of the front page leapt out at him. Friday May 31st, the day the painting was stolen! The thief could have bought this paper on his way to the gallery!

Mitch picked up the painting from his bed. He'd have to take it back first thing tomorrow, but for now he could sit and stare at it.

Five million bucks!

Manhattan Art Gallery, New York.
Friday 7th June, 9.25 a.m.

Mitch's legs felt weak as he forced them up the steps and through the polished wood doors of the Manhattan Art Gallery.

Inside, a crystal chandelier burned brightly. Beneath it, sitting at a small desk, sat a security guard.

The guard looked up lazily as Mitch came towards him. 'Can I help you?' he said.

'Er ...' stammered Mitch.

Why did he feel so nervous? He hadn't done anything wrong. He pulled his rucksack closer to his chest. Inside, he could feel the painting, now back in its newspaper wrapping.

The security guard was waiting, chewing gum. 'Yeah?'

'The ... the picture that got stolen ...' began Mitch.

Instantly, the guard's chewing stopped. His eyes narrowed. 'What about it?' he said.

Mitch put a hand on the clip of his rucksack and opened the top of his bag to reveal the edge of the gilded frame.

'I think I've got it here,' he said, lifting it out a fraction.

For a moment, the security guard looked stunned. Then he snatched up a phone from the wall behind him and punched a couple of buttons. The guard spoke urgently, words Mitch didn't catch. Then, before he knew it, Mitch found his arm clamped in the guard's strong grip.

'OK, son. No problem. Let's have Ms O'Connell take a look at it, huh?'

As Mitch went with the security guard along a short corridor, he felt as if he was being half-led and half-marched until the guard abruptly stopped at a door marked 'PRIVATE'. He knocked, and then opened the door, as a female voice called, 'Come in!'

Inside, a smart-looking woman was sitting behind a rosewood desk. Beside her, his collar unbuttoned, sat a man. On the desk between them, Mitch saw, were a batch of artist's sketches.

'Caroline O'Connell,' said the woman, standing up. She didn't smile, simply held out a hand towards the man. 'This is Detective Matthews, of the New York Police Department. And you are?'

Mitch struggled to find his tongue. 'Mitch Zanelli.'

'So,' said the NYPD detective reaching for Mitch's rucksack, 'what you brought in, fella?'

With fumbling fingers, Mitch removed the tiny painting and handed it over. 'I found it,' he said, his voice shaking.

Matthews peeled back the newspaper, took out the painting, then handed it over to Caroline O'Connell. 'This it, ma'am?' he asked.

Mitch held his breath. Was it?

The director of the Manhattan Gallery took the frame. She glanced at the painting for barely a second before looking up at Mitch.

'Exactly where did you find this?' she said.

'Down at the yacht harbour,' said Mitch. 'In a pile of trash boxes.'

'Then I suggest you take it back there,' snapped Caroline O'Connell.

'What?' gasped Mitch.

'You saying it's a fake, then?' said Detective Matthews.

Caroline O'Connell snorted. 'Not a fake. Just a good quality print.'

Mitch felt angry and afraid at the same time. 'I don't know anything about paintings. I found it. I thought it might be the one ...'

He stopped as Detective Matthews took the painting and spoke to the gallery director. 'The *same* picture as the one you lost, Ms O'Connell. That's a big coincidence.'

The mention of the robbery seemed to make Caroline O'Connell wince. 'Not at all,' she said. 'The gallery's loan of the Turner collection has been widely advertised. Every store in New York has been selling prints like that one!'

Detective Matthews shrugged. As Caroline O'Connell picked up the phone on her desk to call the security guard back, he returned the picture to Mitch. 'Thanks anyway, Mitch,' he said, adding with a glance at the gallery Director, 'Take no notice of her. She's a little stressed. Reckon I'd be if I'd just lost something worth five million bucks ...'

Caroline O'Connell had already turned back to the artist's sketches strewn across her desk. Detective Matthews did the same now, leaving

Mitch to return the painting to his rucksack.

'As I was saying, Ms O'Connell,' said the detective, 'the security video was mighty fuzzy, so our artist has used it as a starting point' – the NYPD man pushed one of the sketches towards her – 'and this is the best he's come up with. We'd like to put up a few copies round the gallery, see if it jogs anybody's memory. OK by you?'

Caroline O'Connell sighed, clearly still embarrassed at the whole business. 'If you must.' She looked down at the sketch. 'Is he anyone known to you?'

Mitch saw the NYPD man shrug. 'Nope. We'll feed him into our computer and get it to carry out a match against the hoods on our files. Something may come up.'

As he finished strapping up his rucksack Mitch wanted to shout, *Something has come up!* but the words wouldn't come out. He wanted to say, *I know that guy!*

He couldn't. After the farce with the picture, they wouldn't believe him anyway.

The security guard's hand landed roughly on his arm. 'Come on. Fun's over for one day.'

Outside, Mitch sat down on the gallery steps. He closed his eyes, trying to conjure up the face he'd seen in the sketch. Could it be? Was he right?

Yes, definitely. He was as certain as he could be.

The man they suspected of walking out with a five million dollar painting under his arm was the same man Mitch had helped send his message over the Net to the STARBOARD web site.

Manor House. Saturday 8th June, 8.55 p.m.
Rob called up the STARBOARD home page and clicked on the underlined words 'Current positions'.

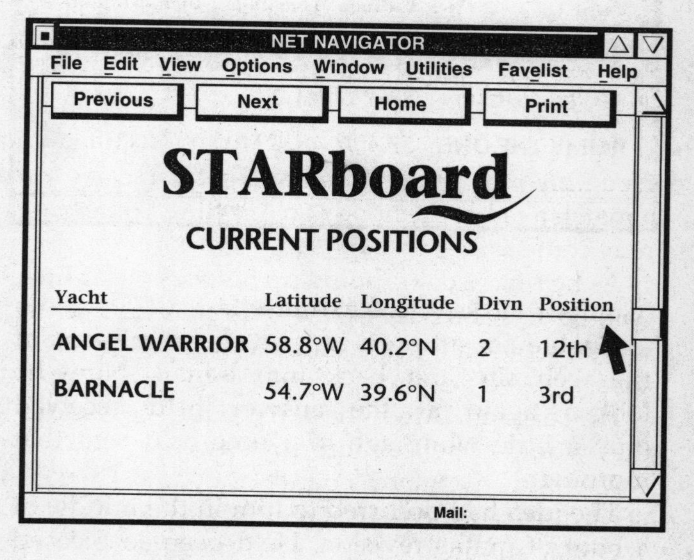

Eagerly he scanned the alphabetical list of yachts. There it was.

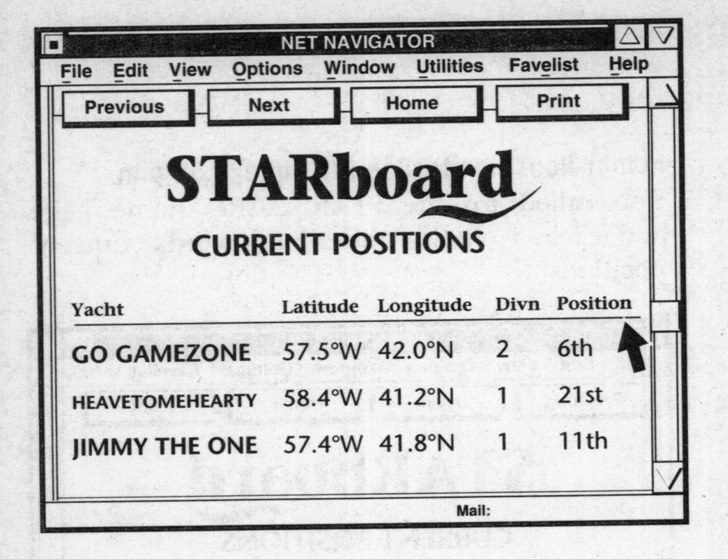

'Going well!' said Rob to himself.

Unable to suppress a grin, he came out of the web site and back into e-mail. Now he looked again at the answer he'd received only a little while ago to a note he'd sent that morning.

The idea had occurred to him in the middle of a bout of maths revision. He'd been so pleased with it he'd broken his vow not to spend any time on the Net until he'd finished revising, and logged in straight away.

And now he'd not only got an answer back – Brad Stewart had said 'yes'!

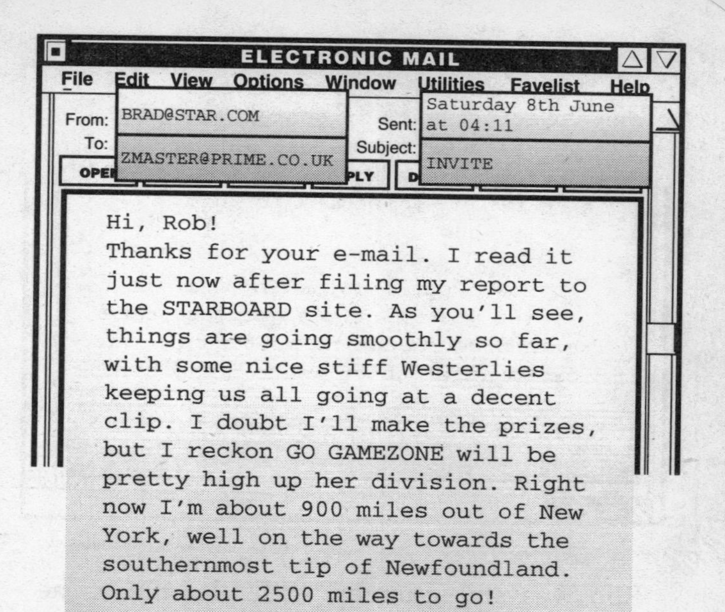

Hi, Rob!
Thanks for your e-mail. I read it just now after filing my report to the STARBOARD site. As you'll see, things are going smoothly so far, with some nice stiff Westerlies keeping us all going at a decent clip. I doubt I'll make the prizes, but I reckon GO GAMEZONE will be pretty high up her division. Right now I'm about 900 miles out of New York, well on the way towards the southernmost tip of Newfoundland. Only about 2500 miles to go!

So, to your question – would I come into Abbey School and talk about the trip? Sure, I'd like that. I can also tell you all about the other things that go on behind the scenes, like all the preparations ... and some of the other daft things like the superstitions I mentioned. There's my superstition about sleeping in a hotel bed, but there's plenty of others – like a guy who was berthed near me in the yacht harbour, for instance. He likes to swap things for the voyage, saying it guarantees both yachts a safe passage. So, he's taking something across for me, and I'm taking something for him. Crazy, huh?

Anyhow, Rob, I'm looking forward to seeing you all. It's going to come as a nice change to meet a big crowd after three weeks on my own!

All the best, Brad Stewart.

Mail:

Rob was still grinning with pleasure as he printed the note. Tamsyn and Josh were coming round that afternoon for a spot of joint revision.

As he tore the copy from the printer, Rob had a change of heart. Maybe he wouldn't say anything this afternoon – or for a while. Maybe he would wait until *GO GAMEZONE* was closer to England and the excitement was really building up. Then it would *really* come as a surprise to them!

Slowly folding the sheet in half, Rob slipped it into the drawer of his desk.

CHAPTER 5

Cyber-Snax.
Sunday 9th June, 9.35 a.m. (UK time 2.35 p.m.)

Mr Lewin looked up as the cafe door buzzed open. 'Mitch? What are you doing here on a Sunday?'

'Hi, Mr Lewin. I want to send a few e-mails, if that's OK?'

Mitch's boss nodded. 'Sure, go on. Say ...' he looked around at the few customers in the café, '... how about you taking care of the place while I go for a little jog?'

'Why not?' said Mitch. 'You go, Mr Lewin. I'll be fine here.'

Mitch settled down at the PC nearest the counter. In between serving coffees and muffins to customers as they came in, Mitch thought more about what to do next.

It had been two days since his trip to the Manhattan Art Gallery. In that time he'd been racking his brains, trying to make some sense of it all.

Who was the guy in the artist's sketch? Was he really involved with the painting robbery? Why did he want to send that message over the Net? It wasn't *his* message, Mitch had realized that. He wouldn't have had it written down on a piece of paper if it had been. But then, if so, who was he sending it to? And why?

So many questions, and he couldn't answer any of them! It was time for team input.

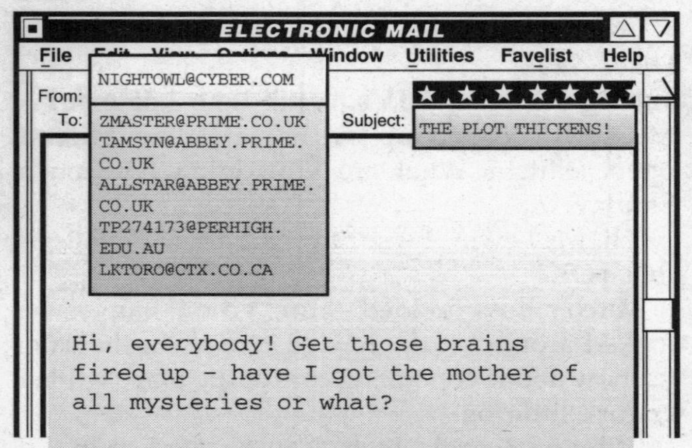

Hi, everybody! Get those brains fired up - have I got the mother of all mysteries or what?

OK, so first you want to know if I'm now a rich dude - yeah? Well, let me tell you right off - I'm not. In fact I came nearer to ending up in the slammer myself!

I took the painting to the boss lady at the Manhattan Gallery. And what did she reckon? It's a dud, worth zilch. She was *not* impressed - and, I can tell you, neither was the NYPD detective she had with her.

Now, here's where it gets interesting. When I got there, the two of them were looking at mug-shots of the guy who walked out with the painting. Well, after the mauling I got I just couldn't bring myself to say anything, but - I've seen him!

He came into Cyber-Snax on Monday morning, just before I set off for the harbour to look round GO GAMEZONE. He wanted to put a message up on the STARBOARD site. Not his message, I don't reckon, coz he had it written down on a sheet of paper and had to keep looking at it. It just seemed a nothing message at the time, but now I'm not so sure.

GOOD SPEED ABOARD CROSSING THE DEEP. BACK SAFE

Mystery number 1, then. Any of you see a clue in there? There's no way I'm going back to the cops until I get an answer!

Mitch 'Puzzled' Zanelli.

OPEN SEND FORWARD REPLY DELETE SAVE PRINT

Mail:

Manor House. Sunday 9th June, 2.45 p.m.

'What are the major exports of Canada?' asked Tamsyn.

Josh leaned towards Rob's PC. 'Hang on, I'll just e-mail Lauren and ask.'

'Good thinking,' said Rob, inching towards the PC as well. 'Maybe she could come over for the exam, too.' He frowned as he looked down at the timetable on his lap. 'She'll have to get her skates on, mind. Geography's on Tuesday.'

'Will you two stop messing about?' said Tamsyn. 'I'm trying to test you. Come on, the major exports of Canada.'

'Wheat, timber, fish ...' said Rob.

'Especially salmon,' added Josh. 'And dead brainy girls named Lauren!'

Tamsyn laughed. 'OK. Now you ask me a question.'

Josh thought for a moment. 'Whereabouts in the Atlantic Ocean is *GO GAMEZONE*?'

'Josh!'

'It's geography, isn't it?' He pointed at the screen of Rob's PC, and the STARBOARD web site display he'd brought up while the other two hadn't been looking. 'And there's the answer.'

In spite of herself, Tamsyn looked. 'Hey, Brad's doing well.' She turned to Rob. 'Have you had any more sea-mail from him?'

Rob paused before answering. 'Er ... no. I expect he's got other things on his mind.'

'Well, nobody else has!' said Josh. 'There's a

bit in the local rag about it every day. And your Dad was on the box last night, wasn't he, being interviewed about *GAMEZONE*'s sponsorship?'

A gentle bleep came from the PC. 'That could be Brad now,' said Josh as MESSAGE WAITING began to flash up on the status line. He reached for the mouse and clicked into the note. Together, they read it in silence.

'So, he didn't find the right one,' said Josh when he had finished. 'I'd have had trouble believing he *had* found the one that was pinched.'

'Me too,' said Tamsyn, 'but don't you think it's odd he found a copy of the *same* painting? That's the weird bit.'

Rob looked mystified. 'So what are you saying? That the painting on show in the gallery was a copy the thief swiped and then dumped when he realized it wasn't a real Turner?'

'It could have been,' laughed Josh. 'Hey, what a cool security system! Fill up your art gallery with dud pictures, and then it doesn't matter if you get burgled – you just put up another dud in its place! All the real paintings are probably stashed underground in a lead-lined vault!'

'Josh, be serious!' Tamsyn moaned. 'We could be on to something here.'

'OK,' said Josh. 'How about this? Mitch's mystery man, whoever he is, sets out to steal the Turner. He's got a copy up his jumper—'

'No, wrapped in a newspaper,' said Rob.

'All right, wrapped in a newspaper,' echoed Josh, 'and his plan is to pinch the real one and put the copy in its place. But when he gets to the art gallery it's late, and he doesn't have time to do the swap. So he just lifts the real one and runs for it. When he's in the clear, he dumps the copy – all ready for Mitch to come along and find.'

Rob flicked his eyes to the ceiling. 'And if you believe that, Tamsyn, you'll believe anything!'

Tamsyn stood up. She ran a hand through her hair, a look of concentration on her face. 'But I *do* believe it! Josh, I think you could be right!'

'What? Seriously?'

'Yes,' said Tamsyn. 'I mean, it's the perfect crime. Nobody comes after you, because you've made it look as if nothing's been stolen!'

Rob held his hands in the air. 'OK, so the guy was planning to do a swap and it didn't work out. He dumps the copy and Mitch finds it. So where does that get us? It doesn't tell us anything about where the painting is now, does it?'

'Maybe that's what the message is about,' said Josh.

They looked at the screen again, at the final lines of Mitch's note.

```
It just seemed a nothing message at the
time, but now I'm not so sure.

GOOD SPEED ABOARD CROSSING THE DEEP.
BACK SAFE
```

'I can't see anything suspicious in it,' said Rob. 'There are dozens like it on the STARBOARD site.'

'Maybe he's just a sailing fan, as well as an art thief,' said Josh.

Tamsyn shook her head. 'I don't believe that either!' She stared at the message. 'It's got to be saying something. If we can only work out what it is.'

Josh turned his head this way and that as he studied the message. 'Safe,' he said. 'Maybe it's saying that's where he's stashed the painting. In a safe!'

'Where it'll be safe, eh?' said Rob. 'Sharp, Josh.'

'What about the rest, though.'

'Deep,' said Josh. 'That could mean ... he's buried the safe the painting's in!'

'And the bit about good speed?' asked Rob.

'That's what he did after burying the safe,' laughed Josh. 'Ran away fast!'

'Come on, guys, take it seriously,' said Tamsyn. 'There could be something in this.' She read the line again. 'Crossing the deep ... What crosses the deep?'

'A bridge?' offered Rob.

'That's a possible,' said Tamsyn. 'There are stacks of bridges in New York. Maybe it's been hidden under one of them.'

'Tamsyn,' said Josh, shaking his head, 'you're thinking of the Mafia. When they pop somebody off they cement 'em *into* a bridge!'

'Don't be so gruesome!' Tamsyn grabbed a sheet of paper. 'Come on then, let's try again ...'

* * *

'That's it,' said Rob an hour later. 'I've had enough.'

The floor was littered with scraps of paper, each with the words of the message written backwards, forwards and in every other direction they could think of. But they were no nearer finding a hidden meaning in it than they were when they'd started.

'It *must* be saying something,' murmured Tamsyn yet again.

'Well, I'm not spending any more time looking for it,' said Rob abruptly, looking at his watch. 'We've got an exam tomorrow, guys. Remember?'

'Exams! Huh!' snorted Josh. 'Come on, Rob, cracking this has got to be more fun than dosing up on the natural resources of Canada!'

'Not until they invent a GCSE in word puzzles it isn't,' said Rob.

'The natural resources of Canada ...' said Tamsyn. 'Well done, Josh. Let's try a couple of them.'

'Huh?'

'Lauren and Allie, of course,' she said. Clicking on FORWARD, Tamsyn typed a short addition to the front of Mitch's note.

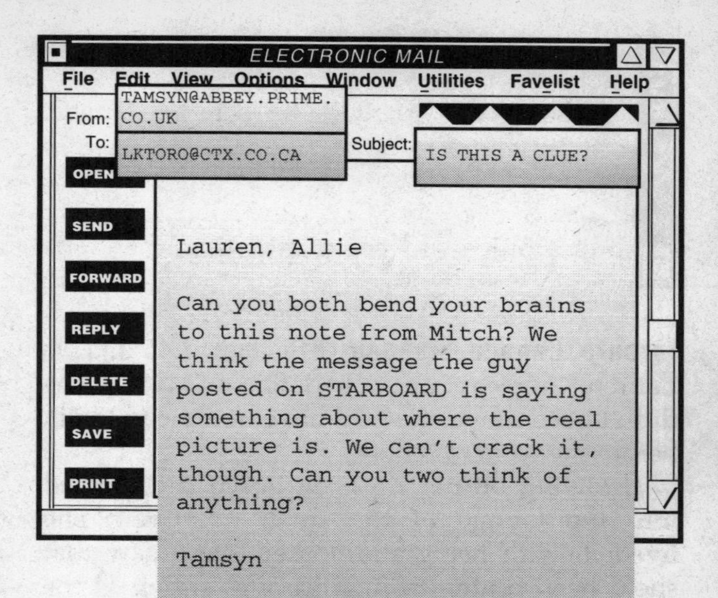

From: TAMSYN@ABBEY.PRIME.CO.UK

To: LKTORO@CTX.CO.CA

Subject: IS THIS A CLUE?

Lauren, Allie

Can you both bend your brains to this note from Mitch? We think the message the guy posted on STARBOARD is saying something about where the real picture is. We can't crack it, though. Can you two think of anything?

Tamsyn

CHAPTER 6

Toronto, Canada. Monday 10th June, 7.45 a.m.

Lauren King leapt out of bed. She was late! If she didn't get a move on she'd have no time to log in before she went to school.

Throwing on her dressing gown she hurried into the lounge of the small apartment she lived in with her grandmother – and saw that she'd been beaten to it. Alice was sitting at the computer in the corner of their lounge, gazing at the screen. On it, Lauren could see a grid of black-and-white squares.

Time for plan A, thought Lauren. 'Allie!' she cried. 'Are we going to have some breakfast today, or what?'

'Soon, honey,' mumbled Alice.

'Is that soon soon, or soon tonight?' asked Lauren.

Alice turned round, her sparkling grey eyes peering over the rims of her spectacles.

'Soon as I get this crossword finished,' she said. 'I found this one after you went to bed. There's an all-expenses paid trip to Niagara Falls going as a prize. Now, you want me to win it for us or not?'

'There'll be no point if I can't go because I'm in hospital recovering from starvation!' cried Lauren.

Alice nodded slowly – then turned back to the screen again. 'Yep, that would be a shame,' she said over her shoulder as she typed in another answer. 'Of course, you could always go fix your own breakfast. It's real easy. You pour some cereal into a bowl and add some milk. Magic!'

'I could make a mess though, Allie. I could spill milk all over myself. Or over the kitchen floor. I could slip on it and crack my head and then you'd have to take me to hospital and spend the day pacing up and down, worrying about me and blaming yourself and …'

'All right, all right!' Alice got to her feet, trying not to laugh. 'You think I don't know you want to check your e-post?'

'E-*mail*, Allie,' laughed Lauren.

'You think I don't know that as well?' Now the old lady did laugh, her finger wagging at the same time. 'Go on with you. But on one condition …'

'What's that?' said Lauren, diving for her chair.

'No e-mail until you've done seventeen down for me. I'm stuck.'

'Allie! Do I have to?'

Alice stopped at the kitchen doorway. 'No … but don't blame me if I can't concentrate in here and come back with a slice of dry bread and a glass of water …'

Settling herself in front of the screen with a

sigh, Lauren looked at the clue for seventeen down. It read:

TAKE IT EASY IN AN IGLOO (5,3)

Another cryptic clue. Two words; the first of five letters, the second of three. Lauren thought hard, but drew a blank.

'I can't do it, Allie!' she called above the clattering and singing that had started up from the kitchen.

Suddenly the serving hatch opened. 'Don't worry, I've got it! "Chill out".'

Lauren looked again at the clue. 'Of course!'

'How about you trying something else?'

'Try something else?' smiled Lauren as the serving hatch snapped shut again. 'Good thinking, Allie.' A click of the mouse and she'd switched across to check her e-mail.

She read Tamsyn's note then, intrigued, quickly read the one from Mitch down to the strange message at the bottom.

GOOD SPEED ABOARD CROSSING THE DEEP.
BACK SAFE

She frowned. It didn't mean anything to her either – except that it looked for all the world like the sort of cryptic clues that Allie had been trying to solve with her crossword.

'How you getting on?' called Allie, opening the serving hatch once more.

Lauren shouted back. 'Not so good.'

'Come on, then. Give us the clue.'

Lauren looked again at the message on the screen. What better test?

'Good speed aboard crossing the deep. Back safe,' she called.

'How many letters?'

'Er … I don't know.'

'Trying to make it tough for me, huh?' said Allie. Moments later Allie replied, 'Well, I've got something. But it doesn't sound right for a crossword. Three word answer, right?'

'How … how d'you work that out?'

Allie came into the lounge, a sheet of paper in her hand. 'Easy,' she said, scribbling as she explained. ' "The deep back" means turn "deep" round – to give "peed".'

'And …' said Lauren slowly, beginning to see what was coming next, ' "crossing peed" means cross out the letters P-E-E-D?'

'Right,' said Alice, 'which leaves the letter "S" to go on to "Good" to make "Goods".' She smiled triumphantly. 'Leaving the three word answer …'

Lauren was ahead of her. 'Goods aboard safe,' she said.

'You got it!' Alice looked at Lauren suspiciously. 'So what number clue was it?'

'It wasn't your crossword clue at all, Allie,' murmured Lauren. 'Forget a hundred dollars. I think you've just cracked a clue to a five million dollar mystery.'

Quickly, she hit the REPLY button …

Abbey School, England.
Wednesday 12th June, 8.25 a.m.

'Goods aboard safe,' breathed Tamsyn as she read Lauren's note. 'Josh, we've got to talk to Rob about this. Have you seen him today?'

They were in the computer room in the Technology Block. What with exams on Monday and Tuesday, it was the first time they'd been able to log in that week.

Josh shook his head. 'He went straight to class Monday and yesterday. He's taking these exams pretty seriously. *Too* seriously if you ask me!'

'Maybe he's sick or something.'

'Yes – with examinitis! He hasn't even mentioned sea-mail since we were round his place on Sunday!'

Tamsyn smiled. Rob had been very quiet lately. But not when he sees *this*, she thought, looking again at Lauren's solution on the screen. 'Goods aboard safe,' she repeated. 'Josh, that can only mean one thing ...'

'That painting's on the way out of the country,' nodded Josh. 'Like the report in the *New York Times* said.'

'On board what, though?' said Tamsyn. 'A plane, or ...'

'A boat?' said Josh. 'Tamsyn, did Mitch say exactly *where* he found that painting?'

'Near the art gallery,' said Tamsyn at once. Then, as she struggled to remember what Mitch had actually said in his first note, doubts flooded into her mind. 'Didn't he?'

Fingers fumbling as he hurried, Josh switched into the mail system and pulled down the first note Mitch had sent them.

```
So, mystery solved - Bruno's the villain.
Mind you, I'm not going to turn in the
mutt. He led me to find a real groovy
painting of an old ship somebody had
thrown out. It's only tiny but it's got
incredible detail.
```

'He doesn't say where he found it,' said Josh.

'But he does!' cried Tamsyn, as she realized the answer. 'He was led to it by that dog, Bruno. And look, higher up the note!'

```
... it was probably set off by a loopy dog
called Bruno that seems to have the run of
the yacht harbour.
```

Tamsyn's eyes were gleaming. 'He found that painting at the harbour.'

'Goods safe aboard,' murmured Mitch. 'Are you saying the painting is on one of the race yachts?'

'Not necessarily. The place was jam-packed according to Mitch. But think about it, Josh. What better way of smuggling it out of the country?'

Josh shook his head. 'They were watching the ports. Didn't the cop say so?'

'But they would have been watching the *passenger* boats, Josh! Not the racing yachts!'

Josh whistled. 'So – how could it have been worked?'

Tamsyn stood up as she thought. There were so many pieces to this, it felt like a jigsaw puzzle. She tried to get things in the right order.

'Let's say we're right, and the real picture was going to be swapped for the copy. So – our thief carries the copy into the art gallery aiming to carry out the switch but he doesn't get time.'

'He just grabs the Turner and runs for it.'

'Down to the yacht harbour, where he gets it on board one of the race yachts and then dumps the copy he hasn't been able to use. Yes?'

'Ye-es,' said Josh slowly.

'You don't sound too convinced.'

'I am,' said Josh. 'But ... *how* did he get it onto one of the yachts?'

Tamsyn searched for an answer. 'I don't know. Maybe he was told where to put it.'

'Who by, though?' asked Josh, looking as though he already had an answer of his own.

'By the person who'd asked him to steal the painting in the first place! Is that what you're getting at?'

Josh nodded, his face unsmiling. 'I think there's more to it than that. Remember Brad Stewart's e-mail? The alarm?'

Tamsyn sat back on her chair again. '*GO GAMEZONE*?' she said, stunned. 'You think the painting could be on *GO GAMEZONE*? As in *that's* why the alarm went off?'

'Because the thief was on board hiding the

stolen painting,' said Josh. 'It all adds up. Brad Stewart found nothing missing ...'

'Because the guy wasn't there to take anything – he was there to hide something instead!"

Tamsyn thought about it for a minute. The alarm *had* gone off the night before the race began – the night of the robbery from the art gallery. The jigsaw was slowly coming together. Or was it? There still seemed to be a piece missing.

'Josh, if the painting's on board *GO GAMEZONE,* then it's on its way here – to Portsmouth. Which means somebody is going to be waiting to collect it at this end. Right?'

Josh nodded. 'The customer. The person who ordered it. The person who asked for it to be stolen.'

'The one who wanted that posting put on the STARBOARD site to tell him "goods aboard safe" ...' said Tamsyn.

'So he'd know,' said Josh, 'that when *GO GAMEZONE* reaches Portsmouth all he has to do is turn up, go on board, and collect.'

The thought, the unbelievable thought, came to Tamsyn at that instant. She tried to sweep it away, but she couldn't. Who would have the perfect opportunity to go on board *GO GAMEZONE* when the yacht arrived?

Her voice was shaking as she said the words. 'Oh, Josh. You don't think the customer could be ... Rob's dad?'

CHAPTER 7

Perth High School, Australia.
Friday 14th June, 12.50 p.m.

'Tom Peterson?'

'Here, Mr Lillee.'

Tom watched as his form tutor marked him present for the afternoon. Good. The first part of his plan had passed off without a hitch – not that he'd have expected otherwise. All he'd had to do was turn up after the lunch break. It was the rest of the plan that was going to give him more trouble.

If the bike thief *was* operating every other Friday, then this was the day the wretch was scheduled to strike again. Tom hoped desperately that he was right. The plan he'd come up with was risky enough as it was; trying it more than once wasn't on. If it didn't work today, then that would be that.

'OK, Kerry?' he whispered to the boy next to him.

Kerry Archer nodded. Tom had persuaded Kerry to cover for him during the afternoon. He agreed at once. Kerry's had been the second bike the thief had taken, after lunch break on Friday 17th May.

After lunch break ... That was another part of the pattern Tom had spotted. His own bike had been in the racks at lunch, because he'd remembered seeing it. He'd checked with Kerry and Debbie Levitt and they'd said the same about their bikes. Every two weeks, sometime during the afternoon ... maybe *this* afternoon ...

As Mr Lillee finished taking the roll, the school bell jangled. All around him, Tom's classmates began grabbing their books and heading off for the first lesson in the Science lab at the far end of the school. Tom and Kerry dawdled behind.

When Kerry gave him a final nod at the classroom door, then turned left for the Science Lab, Tom turned to his right.

He pulled a clipboard from his bag and speeded up. As his dad was always saying, the first rule of surveillance was to make sure you didn't look out of place. If he was stopped by a teacher and asked where he was going, he planned to say he was researching for his project – and hope they didn't then ask 'What project'?

But nobody did stop him. Tom walked briskly down to the end of the corridor and straight past the staff room without looking back. Only when he reached a green cupboard door did he stop and check both ways.

All clear. Quickly, he dipped into his pocket and pulled out the key he'd taken from his mum's handbag that morning. As he unlocked the door and slipped inside, the smell of bleach and polish hit him straight away. Tom's mum had a job as a cleaner at the school, and this was the cupboard in which she kept her cleaning materials. Tom locked the door from the inside, and put the key back in his pocket. So long as it was returned before seven that evening, he'd be all right!

The pungent cupboard smells were the only minus in his plan. They were far outweighed by the two big pluses that the cupboard had going for it. One, a small narrow window up near the ceiling which he could look through without being spotted. And, two, the fact that the window gave him a clear view of the bike racks.

Pushing a stool beneath the window, Tom hopped onto it and looked out. No more than twenty metres away, the row of bikes sat in the sun.

'C'mon then, whoever you are,' muttered Tom. 'You try to have one of them – and I'll have *you*!'

Tamsyn's house, Portsmouth.
Friday 14th June, 7.30 a.m.

Tamsyn put down her French textbook, unable to concentrate. So much for last-minute revision!

For the umpteenth time since she'd looked at Mitch's e-mail with Josh, Tamsyn turned the facts over in her mind. It all fitted together.

But, if they were right, where on *GO GAMEZONE* might the painting be hidden?

They could hardly ask Rob, could they? She couldn't bring herself to believe that the Zanellis were involved, but if they were ...

Of course – Tom! His father must have had dealings with smugglers, gun-running, that kind of thing. Maybe Tom could find out the likeliest hiding place. She'd fire him an e-mail the minute she got to school.

Perth High School, Australia. 3.30 p.m.

Tom crushed his drink can and tossed it hard onto the floor.

Nothing! Not a thing! He'd spent all afternoon in a cupboard, and for what? Not a single, solitary, suspicious movement. If this was what it was like being a detective, then he pitied his dad.

Outside, the school bell began clanging to signal the end of lessons for the day. Tom felt miserable. Nothing was going to happen now, he was sure of that. Any minute now, kids would be pouring out of their classes and charging across to the bike racks.

In fact the first had *already*, Tom was surprised to see. A tall boy, in a maroon Perth High School sweatshirt that looked a size too small for him, had arrived from somewhere to Tom's left and was now walking along the line of bikes. *Quick off the mark or what?* thought Tom.

The boy had found his bike. Casually he pulled it from the rack as other kids, all in their maroon sweatshirts, came racing from the right, across to the bike racks. In moments the youth, slowly wheeling his bike towards the school gates, was surrounded by a whole horde as more and more raced in from Tom's right.

From the right! realized Tom. Frantically, he leapt from the stool and dived for the door. The boy had arrived at the racks from his left! And the only way of reaching the bike racks from that direction was not from any of the school buildings – but by climbing over the perimeter fence!

Abbey School, England.
Friday 14th June, 12.50 p.m.

Tamsyn had hoped for a quick reply to the note she'd sent Tom, but she hadn't expected one quite so fast – or so triumphant!

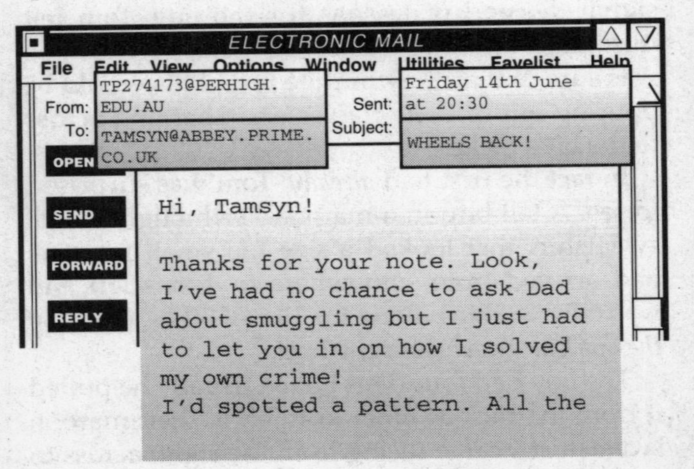
ELECTRONIC MAIL

File Edit View Options Window Utilities Favelist Help

From: TP274173@PERHIGH.EDU.AU
To: TAMSYN@ABBEY.PRIME.CO.UK
Sent: Friday 14th June at 20:30
Subject: WHEELS BACK!

OPEN
SEND
FORWARD
REPLY

Hi, Tamsyn!

Thanks for your note. Look, I've had no chance to ask Dad about smuggling but I just had to let you in on how I solved my own crime!
I'd spotted a pattern. All the

bikes had been nicked on a Friday. So I kept watch all afternoon, today - and caught my bike thief red-handed!
He was a student here a couple of years back. Now he's at work, but he finishes early on Fridays. You know what he was doing? He still had his school sweatshirt, so he was putting it on and climbing over the school fence at going-home time. Bingo - he pinches a bike and walks out the front gate along with the other six million sweatshirt-wearing, bike-pushing kids. No wonder he wasn't spotted!

'Hey, is that neat or what?' said Josh, standing at Tamsyn's shoulder.

SEND
FORWARD
REPLY
DELETE
SAVE
PRINT

Anyhow, I twigged to what was happening and dashed out after him - grabbing a couple of my bigger pals on the way, natch! Next thing the guy knows, we've got him and he's going nowhere. What's more, when the uniforms get round to the guy's place an hour later, they find bikes in every corner - mine included!

Tom 'got my wheels back' Peterson! :-))

Mail:

'Well, I'm glad he's cracked it,' said Tamsyn. 'Even if he hasn't helped *our* investigation.'

'Right,' said Josh. 'Bikes and paintings. Haven't got much in common, have they?'

'Not a lot. You don't get five million dollar bikes.'

Josh grinned. 'Even if you did, it'd be pretty hard to stash one of *them* on *GO GAMEZONE*. It'd stick out like ... like a stolen bike.'

As he said it, Tamsyn turned sharply. 'Josh,' she said quietly, 'maybe Tom *has* helped our investigation.'

'Huh? How?'

'Think about it,' said Tamsyn. 'Suppose that painting's been stashed in a locker. What would happen if Brad Stewart found it? He'd be suspicious at once, wouldn't he? And why – because it would be in the wrong place at the wrong time. Just like everybody at Tom's school would have been suspicious if they'd seen that guy walking out with a bike in the middle of the day when all the kids were in class.'

'Keep going,' said Josh, nodding slowly.

'So ... maybe that painting's not *hidden* on *GO GAMEZONE* at all. Maybe ... it's on show.'

'What ...?' said Josh, barely stopping himself from laughing. 'Hanging up somewhere? In full view!'

But Tamsyn wasn't joking. 'Just like Tom's thief, with his Perth High School sweatshirt. Nobody spotted him before, because he fitted in with the surroundings. He looked as if he was *meant* to be there.'

She looked intently at Josh. 'That yacht's got a smart saloon. What would be *less* suspicious than having a painting hanging up in there?'

'Tamsyn, you're crazy! What would be *more* suspicious than having a painting suddenly turn up where there wasn't one before!'

Tamsyn's face fell. 'I never thought of that.'

'Unless ...' said Josh quietly, 'the same picture *was* there before ...'

'I don't get you.'

'Mitch's copy! What if the idea wasn't to put it in the art gallery in place of the real one? What if the plan was to put the real painting in place of the copy!'

'You mean ...' said Tamsyn, 'the copy was on *GO GAMEZONE*? And the thief swapped it for the real Turner?'

'Setting off the alarm in the process, and dumping the copy as soon as he could – on the quayside, for Mitch to find.'

Tamsyn nodded as she saw what Josh was driving at. 'Leaving a five million dollar painting on board *GO GAMEZONE* that only an expert could tell was any different from the one that had been there all along ...'

She'd hardly finished talking before she was clicking on the SEND button. 'If that painting is there, Mitch may have spotted it when he looked round. Hey, even better ...'

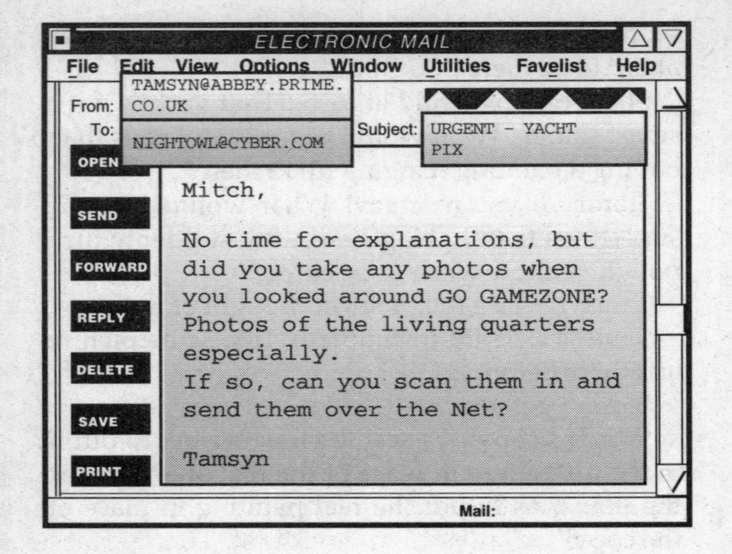

'There is *another* way of checking this out,' said Josh. 'An even better way.'

'How?'

'Remember that CD-ROM Rob showed us?' said Josh hesitantly. 'The one taken by Brad Stewart. That's got a section on it where you get a tour of the yacht.'

'Which could show us if there was a painting hanging in the saloon or somewhere?'

Josh nodded. 'Rob asked me if we wanted to go round there on Sunday and do some revision for the maths exam. Well, while we're there ...'

'We could maybe get a look at that CD-ROM?' Tamsyn took a deep breath. 'But ... if we're right

... if it looks like Mr Zanelli could be involved in this ... Josh, what do we say to Rob?'

'I don't know,' said Josh quietly.

Cyber-Snax, New York.
Friday 14th June, 11.15 p.m.

Mitch had the photographs scanned in and the bitmap files ready. He'd seen Tamsyn's note at the end of his morning stint, but had needed to grab them from home before his evening shift.

He clicked on MAIL SEND and began to type in Tamsyn's e-mail address. Then, as a bright moon came out from behind the clouds and cast its glow into the café, he stopped.

It was Friday, close to midnight. That meant it was early morning in England – and a Saturday. Tamsyn wouldn't be at Abbey School to check these pictures out until Monday. And she'd said she wanted them urgently.

Mitch clicked his fingers as the obvious solution came to him. Tamsyn, Josh – and Rob. Rob had his own machine, didn't he? He'd be sure to log in over the weekend. They were probably checking this out together anyway, and it had just happened to be Tamsyn who sent the e-mail.

Backspacing over Tamsyn's address, Mitch typed Rob's instead. Seconds later, his photos were on their way.

CHAPTER 8

Manor House. Sunday 16th June, 3.45 p.m.

'Mr Zanelli!' gasped Tamsyn.

Rob's father laughed as he held the front door open. 'You don't have to sound so shocked, Tamsyn. I do live here, you know!'

Tamsyn and Josh stepped into the wide hallway, with its polished wood floor. Tamsyn felt her hands shaking as Mr Zanelli took her coat. 'Rob's in his room. You want to go through?'

'Thanks,' said Tamsyn, forcing a smile.

'We'll be having some tea in an hour,' called Mrs Zanelli, popping her head out of the lounge door. 'I hope you've both got room for some.'

'I've *always* got room, Mrs Zanelli,' grinned Josh.

'How can you even *think* about eating?' whispered Tamsyn as they went down the corridor towards Rob's room. 'I feel really nervous about this.'

'Me too,' replied Josh. 'I just don't let my brain tell my stomach, that's all.'

'Hi!' said Rob, flinging open his door. 'I

thought I heard you coming. You're just in time!'

Rob spun his wheelchair round and headed straight over to his computer. Tamsyn and Josh followed him in.

'The latest update on the race,' said Rob pointing excitedly at the screen. 'Brad's doing pretty well!'

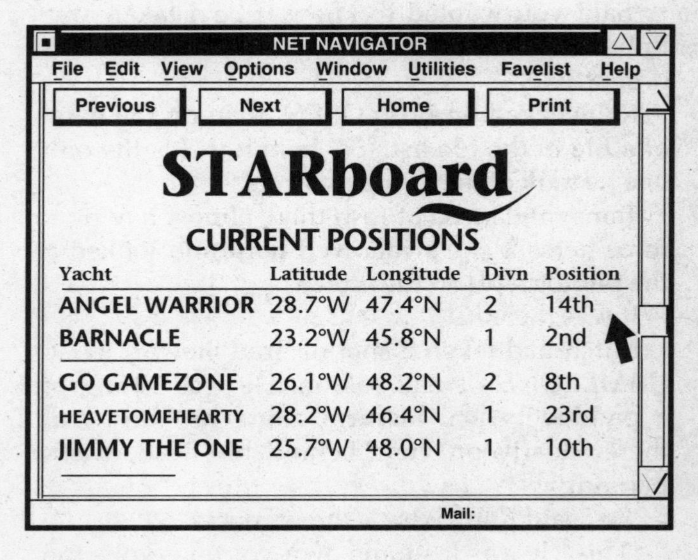

'Eighth? Is that good?' asked Josh.

'It certainly is,' said Rob. 'Their yachts are grouped in different divisions, remember. *GO GAMEZONE* is only a fifty-footer so it's in division two. A bigger one, like ...' Rob scanned the screen, '*JIMMY THE ONE*, that's in division one. And yet Brad's not far behind him.'

He turned to Tamsyn. 'Good, eh?'

Tamsyn smiled weakly. 'Great.' She felt *so* nervous.

Rob seemed not to have noticed, though. Stretching across to the mouse he came out of MAIL and went into his graphics package.

'Mitch sent some bitmaps of *GO GAMEZONE*.'

Tamsyn's heart missed a beat. 'What?'

'Said you wanted to know if he'd taken any.' Rob looked at her. 'And that you were after them urgent-like.'

Rob clicked on FILE OPEN, then on the name of a file in the file list. 'So, here it is. It's the only one he took of the living quarters.'

Tamsyn glanced at Josh then, almost having to force herself, she swallowed hard and looked at the photograph on the screen.

It was there.

Mitch had taken a shot of Brad Stewart in *GO GAMEZONE*'s small saloon. He was sitting on a padded bench, his arm along its back. And there, clearly on view behind his head, was a painting.

'So,' said Rob, 'what's the urgency?'

'This.' It was Josh, his own voice nervous too, now. Leaning across, he dragged the mouse over a section of the screen and then clicked on the 'Zoom' function. Immediately, a larger version of the painting on *GO GAMEZONE* flashed onto the screen. Although the resolution wasn't good, it was clearly a painting of a galleon in full rig.

Rob stared at it. 'Is ... is that what I think it is?'

'The stolen painting?' said Tamsyn grimly.

'Yes, it is. That's why we asked Mitch to send over any shots he'd taken. Rob, that painting's on *GO GAMEZONE*.'

'The copy Mitch found must have been on board all along,' said Josh. 'The thief set the alarm off when he was swapping it for the real one.'

Rob stared at the screen in silence, neither Tamsyn nor Josh knowing what to say to him. When he did speak, it was to surprise them both.

'And you think Brad is ... a smuggler?'

The suggestion hit Tamsyn with a jolt. Brad? The thought of the yachtsman being involved simply hadn't occurred to her.

It was Josh who answered, shaking his head firmly. 'Brad Stewart doesn't know a thing about it.'

'How can you be so sure?' asked Tamsyn.

'Because if he'd been expecting a visitor that night he would have left *GO GAMEZONE*'s alarm off, wouldn't he? No, Rob. The paintings were switched without him knowing. He's just being used to smuggle the real one into this country.'

'Used?' said Rob. 'But – who by?'

As Rob asked the question, Tamsyn and Josh looked at each other. They both looked at the floor, neither of them wanting to voice their suspicions.

They didn't have to. 'My dad!' he said, stunned. 'You think my dad's involved in this, don't you?'

'We ...' Tamsyn struggled to find words, 'we

don't know what to think. But who else ...' Her voice trailed off.

Rob stared at the screen again. 'That might not be *the* painting,' he said. 'It could be *any* painting of a ship. Some other one ...'

'Rob,' said Josh quietly. 'The CD-ROM. That's got shots of below decks on *GO GAMEZONE*, hasn't it? Check that out. It'll be much clearer.'

With fumbling fingers, Rob slipped the CD-ROM into its drive. He brought up the VR program player, selecting to send the video pictures to a screen window rather than the VR headset.

The program opened, not with the buffeting waves and roaring winds that he'd shown Josh, but with the camera taking a leisurely tour of the yacht.

Moving through the cockpit, the image stopped to show the communications equipment and map table, the curtained berths in which crew members would snatch some sleep ... and then finally on into the small saloon.

The clear voice of Brad Stewart came out of the twin speakers as he commentated on what they were seeing. 'If the weather's kind to me on the way across the Atlantic, I may get a chance to put my feet up in here ...'

Slowly, the camera panned around the saloon. With a sudden movement, Rob jabbed at the mouse and put the video into freeze-frame.

'It's not there,' gasped Rob. 'There's nothing there!'

In the spot above the bench seat, the spot

where in Mitch's photograph a painting hung, there was just a blank space.

Rob's mind was in a whirl. How had the painting got there? And when? Could his dad have given it to Brad Stewart when they met in New York and talked about sponsorship? Could it have all been planned? After all, who would be in a better position to pick up a stolen painting when it arrived in Portsmouth than the owner of the company sponsoring the yacht?

'Hey, I don't see much revision going on here. What's the problem – waiting for some food to power you up?'

Rob swung round. 'Dad ...'

Mr Zanelli smiled as he saw what they were watching. 'A good CD, huh? Got a lot of potential. I'm glad Brad took up my suggestion of a gentle tour of the yacht before all the action stuff. He'd never considered it.'

Rob glanced at the screen and back to his father. 'Never ... You mean the tour shots were your idea? They hadn't been taken when you met him in New York?'

Mr Zanelli shook his head. 'No. He just had the sailing bits. What you're looking at there was only filmed a couple of weeks ago.' Mr Zanelli swung open the door again. 'Anyway, your mother says to tell you it's tea in ten minutes. Don't be late.'

As the door closed, Rob didn't know whether to laugh or cry. 'Did you hear that?' he said, waving the CD. 'Two *weeks* ago. That painting wasn't on board two weeks ago – and Dad hasn't been to the States for two *months*!'

Josh broke into a grin. 'So he couldn't possibly have been the one who planted it.'

Tamsyn gave a huge sigh of relief. 'Rob, I'm *so* pleased!'

Rob's joy was short-lived. Grimly he brought Mitch's bitmap photograph back onto the screen. 'But somebody did. Somebody put that painting on *GO GAMEZONE* recently. The question is: who?'

'And why?' added Josh. 'That's the bit I don't understand. Why go to all the hassle of planting it on *GO GAMEZONE*?'

'In case anything goes wrong, of course!' said Tamsyn. 'He's letting Brad take the risk for him!'

Josh whistled. 'You're right. If that painting *is* found on *GO GAMEZONE* when it arrives in Portsmouth next week, Brad Stewart's sure going to have a lot of explaining to do.'

Explaining?

At the mention of the yachtsman's name, Rob yanked open the drawer of his desk. Pulling out the e-mail he'd been keeping as a surprise for the past fortnight, he rapidly read it again.

'There ... there!' he cried, pointing at the paragraph which had just shot out of his memory like a laser beam.

```
There's my superstition about sleeping in
a hotel bed, but there's plenty of others
- like the guy who was berthed next to me
in the yacht harbour, for instance. He
```

```
likes to swap things for the voyage,
saying it guarantees both yachts a safe
passage. So, he's taking something across
for me, and I'm taking something for him.
Crazy, huh?
```

'That's how it was done!' shouted Rob.

Tamsyn tried to take in what she was reading. 'You mean ...' she said slowly, 'Brad was *given* the copy of the painting?'

'Yes!' said Rob. 'And then it got swapped for the real one the night of the robbery!'

'But – why?' asked Tamsyn. 'Why go to all the hassle of using a copy? Why not just give him the real painting straight off?'

'Because Mr X wasn't to know that the robbery wouldn't be reported at once. He had to think of a way that wouldn't make Brad suspicious – and what would be better than giving him the painting *before* the real one was stolen!'

'But now the real one is what Brad's carrying,' said Josh. 'And when he turns up in Portsmouth he'll just hand it back ...'

'To Mr X!' said Tamsyn. She looked at Rob and Josh, her eyes glittering. 'That's where he is! That's why the thief Mitch saw in Cyber-Snax was posting his message to the STARBOARD site – so that it could be read by Mr X!'

'So ... Mr X could be in the race?' said Josh. 'Sailing one of the yachts?'

'Yes!'

Rob glanced across to the map on his wall, and

at the cluster of pins which were getting closer and closer to the English coast.

'Then we've got no more than five days to work out who he is,' he said.

'Five days?' said Josh. 'We don't need five minutes, do we? All we've got to do is e-mail Brad and ask him what he was given ...'

'And who gave it to him,' said Tamsyn quickly. 'Josh is right.'

Rob looked doubtful. 'Yes, but ... how do we say that in an e-mail? "Brad, we think you've been tricked into smuggling a five million-dollar painting into the country – who did you get it from?" '

'Basically ... yes,' said Tamsyn. 'But not like that. Like this ...'

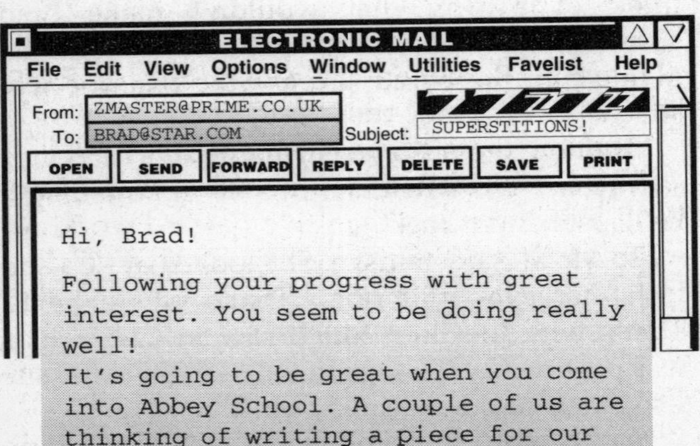

ELECTRONIC MAIL

File Edit View Options Window Utilities Favelist Help

From: ZMASTER@PRIME.CO.UK
To: BRAD@STAR.COM
Subject: SUPERSTITIONS!

OPEN SEND FORWARD REPLY DELETE SAVE PRINT

Hi, Brad!

Following your progress with great interest. You seem to be doing really well!
It's going to be great when you come into Abbey School. A couple of us are thinking of writing a piece for our school newsletter telling everybody about your visit.

'Are we?' said Rob.

'We are now!' Josh answered.

```
Your idea about giving the
background is brilliant. It will
be really interesting - especially
the superstitions. The one you
mentioned about swapping things
with another yachtsman was a cool
example. What did you give him to
carry over, and what did he give
you? Who is he, by the way - which
yacht is he sailing?

Rob.
```

Mail:

'Not bad,' said Rob, impressed. 'Not bad at all.'

Tamsyn clicked on the SEND button. 'Well, let's hope it does the trick.'

'And if it doesn't?' said Josh.

'Then,' replied Rob, 'it'll be worse than I said. We'll have even *less* than five days to work out who this Mr X really is.'

CHAPTER 9

The Atlantic Ocean.
Monday 17th June, 00.10 a.m.

Brad Stewart looked at the weather map on his PC screen and gave a grunt of satisfaction. *At this rate we'll be in Portsmouth by Saturday lunch-time.*

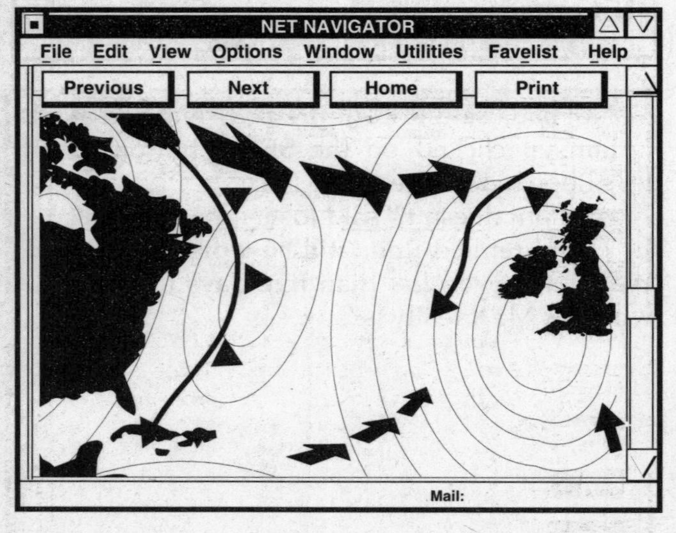

He turned to the radar display by his side. At the top, the south-west tip of the coast of

Ireland was just in view.

Climbing out from the cockpit and on to the rear deck, he looked up at the swollen sails, then out across the vast, dark, heaving ocean. The conditions were perfect: a good westerly wind, with no hint of a storm brewing up.

He gave another nod of satisfaction. There was no need for him to take control from the auto-pilot for a while yet. Pausing only to check the yacht's bearings, he went back to his PC.

It was as he switched off the weather reports provided on the STARBOARD site that he came across Rob's e-mail. He looked at his watch.

'Right. Reply to Rob, then it's a couple of hours shut-eye.'

He clicked on the REPLY button.

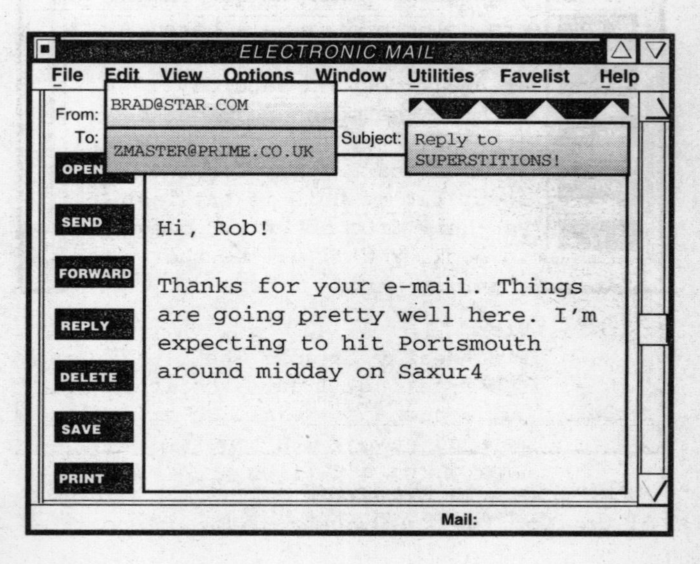

'What the ...' exclaimed Brad as odd characters suddenly appeared on his screen. As he watched, a couple of others popped up in equally odd places.

'Come on,' he muttered. 'Don't give up on me now.'

He cancelled the note, quit the system, then brought it up again. This time, everything looked fine. He typed quickly.

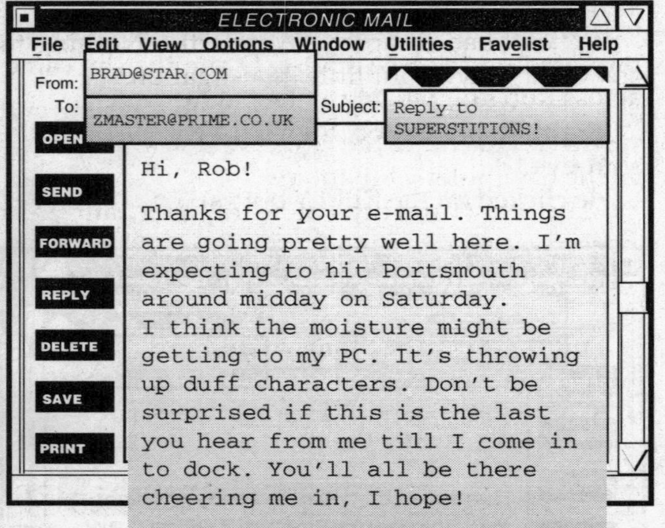

As he clicked on SEND, it was as if he'd triggered off a storm. Letters changed and popped up everywhere on his screen.

And then it went blank.

Abbey School. Tuesday 18th June, 8.25 a.m.

'An exam-free zone!' said Josh brightly as he met Tamsyn outside the Technology Block. 'Doesn't it feel great?'

Tamsyn had to agree. 'Wonderful. Nothing to get in the way of our little investigation.'

They pushed through the double doors and down to the end of the corridor. Rob was already in the Computer Club room.

'Any reply from Brad Stewart?' said Tamsyn at once.

Rob nodded grimly. 'Yeah – for all the good it is.'

Pulling up chairs, Tamsyn and Josh sat beside him. They saw at once what Rob was on about.

'Gee,' said Josh. 'More of a mess than a message.'

to hit Porjsmouph around midsay on
Sar8rd(y.

I thin3 the mois5ure mifht be get&ing
to my PC. It's thr^wing up d3ff
charact2rs. Don't be su\pri=ed
if this is the last yyu hear from
me(twll I com> in to do$k. You'll
jll be th4r% chwqcing me in, I hopt!

Bjad
P.S. Negruy forgzr. ghe supzcgyitio>.
I6gabe tue ottir kuy7a pqckst
c7mp8[s. He gsve me a pa3nt+\8. Gis
lgne's ypm Gxliqy. H$'s sssli3g a
zqcht c=@12d #wMq0 zmi Ojr.

ZZZZ Mail:

'The first bit's not so bad,' said Rob. 'He's having trouble with his PC.'

'That would explain the jumble,' said Josh. 'Whatever's going wrong is changing bits in the ASCII codes.'

'Huh?' said Tamsyn. 'What's that in English?'

'Characters are stored in the computer as codes of ones and noughts. They must be getting changed around.'

'So can't we change them back?'

Josh shook his head. 'No way. They'll be changing randomly. All we can do is guess what the message says.'

Rob pointed at the bottom of Brad Stewart's

note. 'Trouble is, that's the important bit – and there's no guessing what *any* of that says.'

'I don't know,' said Tamsyn. 'Look at the first bit. Doesn't that say "I gave the other guy a packet something"?'

```
P.S. Negruy forgzr. ghe supzcgyitio>.
I6gabe tue ottir kuy7a pqckst c7mp8[s.
```

Rob and Josh looked closely.

'Could be,' said Rob. 'The trouble is, how do we know which characters should be there, and which have been mucked up?'

'We don't,' said Josh. 'But Tamsyn could be right. That bit could say "packet" something. Or "pocket" something.'

'Pocket compass!' said Rob. 'That would make sense. It's the sort of thing a yachtsman would have.'

```
He gsve me*a pa3nt+\8.
```

They looked at the next part. ' "He gave me a painting",' cried Tamsyn. 'That last word's just *got* to say "painting"!'

Josh looked sceptical. 'Painting? How d'you work that out?'

'You sure that's not what you *want* it to say, Tamsyn?' said Rob. 'It's only got four of the right letters. The other four are wrong.'

'Yes, but they're *obviously* wrong, aren't they?' said Tamsyn fiercely. 'I mean, we can forget about the seven, the three and the right bracket and the hash, can't we?' She snatched a piece of paper from her shoulder bag and scribbled the word down, with asterisks in place of the bad characters she'd just mentioned.

pa*nt***

'It *could* say "painting",' said Rob. 'It could *also* say "paintpot".'

But Josh was convinced. 'Even when we know the yacht's recently had a painting put on it? 'Tis good enough for me, Rob. That word was "painting" when Brad typed it.'

He turned to the final part of the e-mail. 'But there's no way of working out what this next lot says!'

```
Gis lgne's ypm Gxliqy. H$'s sssli3g a
zqcht c=@12d #wMq0 zHi Ojr.
```

Tamsyn stared hard at the final two sentences, trying to mould it into some sort of shape in her mind's eye. It was hopeless.

'There's hardly a single word that looks like anything,' she said.

Rob turned to the other two. 'Come on, let's think about this logically. What would we have written if we'd been in Brad's position?'

'This is starting to sound like another exam,' said Josh, 'and there's me thinking we'd finished with them.'

'Josh, that's it!' said Tamsyn. 'That's what we'd have done. We'd have answered the questions as if it was an exam. In order! The order we asked him our questions!'

Rob stared at the letter jumble. 'So somewhere buried in that lot is … two names?'

'The guy he did the swap with, and the yacht he's sailing,' said Tamsyn. 'Yes.'

'Yacht, yacht, yacht,' said Josh immediately. 'Look at the fourth word in the second sentence: "zqcht". Couldn't that have been "yacht"?'

'Right,' said Tamsyn. 'So that bit could have been, "He's sailing a yacht called".' She began writing furiously on the scrap of paper. 'Yes, it matches up. Look.'

He's sailing a yacht called
H$'S sssli3g a zqcht c=@12d #wMqY zHi Ojr

'It doesn't help us with the name of it though, does it?' Josh said.

'No,' said Rob. 'But what it does mean is that the part before it tells us the guy's name.'

```
Gis lgne's ypm Gxliqy.
```

'Hey,' cried Tamsyn, scribbling again. 'If it started off with "his name's" …'

His name's
Gis lgne's ypm Gxliqy

'Then those end two words could be it!' said Josh. He shook his head and sighed. 'But ... that just leaves us in the same position. We can't work out what his name is because we don't know which of those letters is correct and which isn't!'

Rob snapped his fingers. 'So why don't we have the Net do the work?'

Within moments he'd switched to the STARBOARD home page with its short menu of options. At the bottom of the menu was an extra entry: KEYWORD SEARCH. Rob clicked on it. Immediately a panel popped up:

```
SEARCH FOR?
```

Rob typed in: G#####

'What on earth does that mean?' said Tamsyn.

'It's asking the system to search for names starting with a "G" and followed by any five characters, whatever they are,' said Rob. He set the search into motion.

Almost at once the result flashed up.

```
Search for G###### - 2 matches found:
LEN GARRET sailing WINDSONG
JAMES GILROY sailing JIMMY THE ONE
```

'OK, now we try it again,' said Rob, 'but this time with just the second character.'

Returning to the SEARCH FOR? panel, he typed in: #x####.

```
Search for #x#### - 0 matches found
```

'I get it,' said Tamsyn. 'So we do it for each character.'

Rob nodded. The next three searches each turned up blank. Then, finally, he tried searching on: #####y

```
Search for #####y - 1 match found:
JAMES GILROY sailing JIMMY THE ONE
```

'James Gilroy,' said Tamsyn. She pulled her sheet of paper towards her. 'Or ... *Jim* Gilroy! Look, it matches!

His name's Jim Gilroy
Gis lgne's ypm Gxliqy

'And the yacht!' cried Rob, looking at the sentence following. 'So does that!

He's sailing a yacht called JIMMY THE ONE
H$'S sssli3g a zqcht c=@12d #wMqY zHi Ojr

Tamsyn pointed at the search result on the screen. 'Why is "Gilroy" underlined? Doesn't that mean there's more information somewhere?'

'Yes, it does,' said Rob. Moving the mouse across to the underlined name, he clicked once. This time, instead of an immediate response, there was a long delay.

'What's going on?' asked Tamsyn.

'It must be trying to connect through to another computer on the Net,' said Josh. 'The one that's holding some more information about him ...'

At that moment, the screen display changed. 'It was!' cried Tamsyn. 'It was transferring to an entry in an on-line copy of a business directory.'

Gilroy, James Michael: Financier.
b. Manchester, England. 13 May 1947.
Educ. Wrighton Grammar School and City of London University, London.

'And look! At the bottom!' At the end of a string of jobs and business achievements, there were some further paragraphs.

Sports: James Gilroy has a passion for all forms of racing. He owns a string of racehorses, stabled at Newbury in Berkshire. He also owns a 60-foot racing yacht, JIMMY THE ONE, which he regularly enters for races around the world. Gilroy is a fine sailor in his own right, having competed in a number of single-handed races.

'We know about the yacht,' said Rob.

'But we didn't know about *that* lot,' said Josh, pointing.

Other Interests: Fine Art is a second passion for James Gilroy. He invests in many areas, in particular porcelain, antiques and paintings.

His collection of paintings is one of the finest private collections in the country.
Unfulfilled Ambitions: He has two. 'To win the Derby with one of my racehorses,' he says, 'and to complete the *Times* crossword in less than twenty minutes!'

'It's all there,' said Rob. 'He collects paintings ...'

'And he's into crossword puzzles,' said Josh, remembering the message on the web site that Lauren and Allie cracked.

A further memory stirred in Tamsyn's brain. 'Didn't Mitch say something else in his note? About some guy who gave him aggro when he went to look over *GO GAMEZONE*?'

Rob shrugged. 'I don't remember that.'

'Did you file the note?' asked Josh.

'But of course!' said Rob. The e-mail was retrieved – and they saw that Tamsyn was right.

That's not why the alarm went off, though. Brad reckons it was probably set off by a loopy dog called Bruno that seems to have the run of the yacht harbour. I agree with him. Anybody else would have had to get past a skinhead called Gilroy who was on the next-door yacht. The guy was ready to clap me in irons till Brad told him I was on the level.

'It *was* Gilroy,' said Josh. 'And maybe that's why he was so jumpy – because by then he'd have seen that posting on the Net and would have known the stolen painting was on board *GO GAMEZONE.*'

'Let me get this straight. At some point after they get into Port Solent, Brad is going to hand that painting over to this Jim Gilroy?'

'Not knowing it's been swapped and the one he's handing over is actually worth five million bucks,' said Rob. 'Right.'

'So why don't we just tell the police now? Or even keep watch and steam in at the moment when Gilroy's taking delivery?'

'Because he'd deny everything,' said Tamsyn. 'That's why he's been so clever. If anything goes wrong, the suspicion all falls on Brad Stewart.'

'And my Dad ...' said Rob.

The three friends fell silent. They'd worked out what must have happened, and who was responsible. Now, each of them was thinking the same thought.

It was Josh who spoke it aloud. 'So what do we do now?'

'Well,' said Tamsyn. 'There *is* a way. It'll all depend on Mitch, though ...'

CHAPTER 10

New York, USA. Tuesday 18th June, 10.10 a.m. (UK time 3.10 p.m.)

Mitch handed the padded envelope to the mail clerk, only two hours after he'd seen Rob's emergency e-mail. The theory they'd come up with pointing to Gilroy as the mastermind behind the whole business seemed pretty convincing.

But why had Rob asked him to send this? He looked again at the bulging, strongly taped-up envelope as the mail clerk weighed it on a set of scales . Mitch had no idea.

'How long will it take to get there?' he asked the clerk.

'Depends. We do a whole range of services. We can get it there in a day, we can get it there in a month.'

'Shee!' whistled Mitch. 'Talk about snail-mail!'

'Huh?'

Mitch shook his head. 'It's OK. When you're used to firing off e-mails that get where they're going in seconds, then even a day seems kinda slow.'

'Well a day's the best we can do,' said the clerk.

He pointed down to a list taped to the counter. ' "Gold Express". That's our top speed service.'

'And top whack!' gasped Mitch as he saw that the price was way above the amount he'd brought with him. 'I can send an e-mail for a couple of cents!'

The clerk lifted the padded envelope off the scales. 'Yeah, well, until they work out a way of squeezing one of these down a telephone wire, you're gonna have to make do. So, which service d'you want?'

Mitch checked down the list until he found one he could afford. 'How long will it take that way?'

'Bronze service? Three days, minimum.'

'Three days ... so it should be there by Friday OK.'

The clerk solemnly put the envelope into a sack behind his counter. 'Not should be. Could be. If you're lucky.'

Manor House. Friday 21st June, 7.24 a.m.

Rob was opening the front door even before the postman knocked.

'Hi,' he said brightly, his eyes fixed on the pile of mail in the postman's hand.

'Not your birthday, is it?' laughed the postman. 'I hope not. There's nothing looking like a card in this lot.'

'Nah,' said Rob. 'Just saw you coming, that's all.'

Calmly, Rob took the pile of mail. As soon as

he'd closed the door, though, all signs of calm disappeared as Rob began rifling through the pile as quickly as he could.

Ignoring the letters completely, he went straight for the three thick, padded envelopes at the bottom of the pile.

'Mr P. Zanelli,' he muttered as he saw who the first was addressed to. He lifted up the second. 'Mrs Theresa Zanelli.' It *had* to be the third one.

It was larger than the other two. Just the right sort of size. Slowly, Rob turned it over. American stamps! He looked at the address label …

Mr Paul Zanelli,
Managing Director, GAMEZONE LTD.

It wasn't the one. Mitch's package hadn't arrived.

Port Solent, Portsmouth.
Friday 21st June, 3.50 p.m.

'What are we going to do if it doesn't turn up tomorrow?' said Tamsyn.

Rob shook his head. 'Think of another plan,' he said. 'And fast …'

He was interrupted by Josh, hissing as he looked through the binoculars he'd brought with him, 'There it is! *JIMMY THE ONE!*'

They'd persuaded Mrs Zanelli to drop them off at Port Solent after picking Rob up from school. According to the Net info, there were a couple of yachts arriving that afternoon.

Settled in the ideal spot for watching the boats tie up, they looked on as the sleek yacht drew closer, its sails down and its engine chugging.

'Is that him?' whispered Tamsyn, as *JIMMY THE ONE* came close enough for them to make out the swarthy man at the helm.

'Must be, he's got no hair,' said Rob.

'Lights. Action!' murmured Josh, beside them. He lifted the Abbey School video camera to his eye. 'I'd better get *some* shots of a yacht coming in,' he said, pressing the red button at the side.

Tamsyn and Rob stayed quiet as Josh filmed *JIMMY THE ONE* cruising past them and being eased expertly alongside the quay.

'He doesn't look like a crook,' said Rob, staring at Gilroy.

'What did you expect?' said Tamsyn. 'Hooped jersey and a mask, with a bag marked "swag" over his shoulder?'

'Wait until you see this close-up,' said Josh, zooming in on Gilroy before pressing the start button again. 'With his face, a mask would be an improvement!'

They watched, and Josh filmed, until *JIMMY THE ONE* had been tied up and Gilroy registered by race officials.

'Well at least now we know what he looks like,' said Tamsyn.

'And ...' said Rob, pointing a little further along the jetty, 'we know where we'll be tomorrow.'

Tamsyn followed his line of sight. A little

further along from Gilroy's yacht, there was an empty berth.

'That's just got to be *GO GAMEZONE*'s berth,' continued Rob. According to the Net info, Brad Stewart's the next one due in.'

'Tomorrow morning,' added Tamsyn.

'What time?' asked Josh, packing the video camera away.

'About ten,' said Rob. 'Mum says we've got to leave at half-nine on the dot to make sure we're here in time.'

'And what time does the postman arrive?'

Rob gave her a wry smile. 'On a Saturday? Round about half-nine.'

Manor House. Saturday 22nd June, 9.29 a.m.

'Rob!' called Mrs Zanelli, 'what are you waiting for?'

'The post!' shouted Rob. 'I'm expecting something from Mitch.'

'It'll have to wait until we get home. Brad will be sailing back to New York by the time we get there!'

At the front gate of Manor House, Rob looked out along Oaklands Avenue. There was still no sign of the postman.

'Come on, Rob!' shouted Mr Zanelli, lifting up the hatch of their estate car.

Slowly, Rob turned his chair round and pushed himself back towards the car. As Mrs Zanelli helped him into the back seat, Rob's father folded down his wheels and humped them into the luggage area.

'Where are we picking up Josh and Tamsyn?' asked Mrs Zanelli, climbing into the driving seat and starting the engine.

'Southampton Road,' said Rob glumly. 'At the roundabout.'

Swinging the car into a three-point turn, Mrs Zanelli moved off down the driveway ... and stopped. 'Now where's your father gone to?'

Instead of waiting to close the front gates and jump into the passenger seat, Mr Zanelli had vanished.

With a mutter of 'Typical ...' Mrs Zanelli swung the car out into the road and climbed out to shut the gates herself. She was just climbing back into the driving seat as Mr Zanelli came running down the road – a pile of envelopes and packages in his hand.

'Saw him come round the corner,' he puffed, jumping into the car.

'Anything for me?' asked Rob anxiously.

Mr Zanelli didn't look round. 'Plenty of bills if you want them,' he said. Then he turned round. 'But I expect you'll settle for this.'

In his hand was a padded envelope.

By the time they stopped to pick up Tamsyn and Josh, Rob had ripped open the envelope.

Without a word, the three friends gazed at what was inside ... at the final piece in their plan.

Mitch's copy of the stolen Turner painting had arrived.

Port Solent, Portsmouth. 9.47 a.m.

They heard the distant ripple of applause begin as Mrs Zanelli turned their car into its reserved parking spot. Far out, at the mouth of the harbour, its white hull glinting in the sun, *GO GAMEZONE* was heading their way. On the horizon, another boat was just visible.

'You go on ahead,' said Rob to his parents once he was in his chair. 'We'll catch up.'

'OK,' said Rob when they'd gone, 'have we got everything?'

Josh lifted the video camera. Tamsyn held up the padded envelope with Mitch's worthless painting inside. 'Everything,' she said. 'Now all we need is a bit of luck.'

CHAPTER 11

Rob, Tamsyn and Josh followed Mr and Mrs Zanelli onto the quay. There was quite a crowd watching, together with a local television crew who had set up their equipment to get the best shots of *GO GAMEZONE*'s arrival.

By the second, the miniature yacht they'd seen way out at the harbour mouth when they'd arrived loomed larger and larger. Soon it was close enough for them to see Brad Stewart waving from the deck.

'Gilroy!' whispered Tamsyn. 'There he is!'

Further down the quay, legs dangling idly over the side of his yacht, was Jim Gilroy. He had a folded newspaper on his lap, but he wasn't reading it. He was watching the new arrival too.

'Keeping a close eye on things, isn't he?' said Josh.

'Which is what you'd expect if we're right,' said Rob. It was time to check that out for sure. 'Ready, Tamsyn?'

Out in the harbour, *GO GAMEZONE* was no more than five minutes away. It had to be now. Tamsyn nodded nervously. 'I'm ready.'

Leaving Josh to keep Rob's parents occupied with non-stop questions, Tamsyn pushed Rob along the quay to where Jim Gilroy was still sitting, still watching.

'Hi!' called Rob as they drew level with *JIMMY THE ONE*. 'You must be Jim Gilroy.'

The yachtsman looked down at them from the deck, but didn't speak.

'We've been reading about you,' called Tamsyn. 'We've been following the race on the Internet. Sending e-mail to Brad Stewart.'

'Good for you,' said Gilroy.

Rob took a deep breath. This was it – the big test.

'Brad was telling us about your superstition ...'

'What about it?' said Gilroy sharply.

Rob's heart leapt. *So we were right! Brad's e-mail* was *talking about him!*

'Just ... about it,' said Rob coolly. 'Exchanging things. Real interesting.'

Gilroy got to his feet. 'Yeah. Well, if you'll excuse me, kid, I've got things to do.'

'That's a bonus,' whispered Tamsyn as Gilroy strutted to the stern of *JIMMY THE ONE* and disappeared below deck. 'We may have scared him off for a while.'

Rob swung round and headed back along the quay. 'I reckon he'll wait until the fuss has died down anyway,' he said. Ahead of them the TV crew had now been joined by a clutch of newspaper reporters, some of whom were already asking Mr and Mrs Zanelli questions and jotting down answers in their notebooks.

'Phew, it's all happening,' said Josh, coming to meet Rob and Tamsyn.

'With a lot more to come,' said Rob. 'We hope!'

The next half-hour passed very quickly as they watched Brad Stewart manoeuvre *GO GAMEZONE* into her berth, then be officially registered by the race organizers amidst a furious clicking of cameras recording the scene for the local papers. Only after Mr and Mrs Zanelli had completed a TV interview alongside Brad did the crowd start to disperse.

'Ready?' whispered Rob to Tamsyn and Josh. 'I think this is it.'

Tamsyn and Josh nodded. Ceremonies over, Rob's parents were guiding Brad Stewart across towards them.

'Brad,' said Mr Zanelli, 'meet Rob, Tamsyn and Josh.'

'Hey, me and Rob are old pals,' said Brad Stewart at once. 'We've been meeting in cyber-space for weeks!' He grinned. 'Well, until a couple of days ago, anyhow, when my PC went on the blink.'

They all shook the yachtsman's hand. Rob hesitated. This part *had* to work. 'Brad ... we were wondering ... any chance of having a look aboard *GO GAMEZONE*?'

'Now?' said Brad.

'It'd be really cool,' said Josh.

The yachtsman grinned. 'Sure, why not!' He turned to Mr and Mrs Zanelli. 'Won't you join

me? I've got a bottle of champagne I've been saving for when I got here. Why don't we go and crack it open by way of celebration?'

To Rob's relief, Mr and Mrs Zanelli agreed at once. As Brad and his father helped him from his wheelchair and carried him aboard between them, Rob sneaked a glance across at *JIMMY THE ONE*. Gilroy was back on deck, watching their every move.

'Make yourselves comfortable,' said Brad Stewart, as they all squeezed onto the bench seats. 'Though there's a lot more room with just one on board.'

'We can't wait for you to tell us what that's been like, Brad,' said Mrs Zanelli.

'Er ...' said Rob. 'I think you might have to, Mum.' He looked at Tamsyn and Josh. 'We have to tell you all something first.'

'Tell us something? About what?'

Rob pointed above her head, at the small painting hanging just where Mitch's photograph had shown.

'About that painting ...' said Rob.

It was nearly an hour later before Brad and Mr and Mrs Zanelli were helping Rob back down the gangplank and into his wheelchair. 'Are you sure this will work?' said Mr Zanelli.

Glancing over towards *JIMMY THE ONE*, Rob saw Jim Gilroy reappear then, as he saw that Brad Stewart wasn't alone, slip back out of sight.

'I think so. It's got to be worth a try.'

'If anything goes wrong ...' said Mrs Zanelli.

Rob didn't need her to finish. It had been hard enough convincing them all that the painting Brad had carried 3500 miles across the Atlantic was stolen, but even harder getting them to agree to Rob's plan.

'It won't. All three of you will be watching. When Gilroy moves, you move. No problem.'

They looked uncertain. Finally Mrs Zanelli said, 'All right.'

Rob gave another glance across to *JIMMY THE ONE*. Gilroy was looking at them all right, half-hidden in his yacht's cockpit. It was time.

'Tamsyn! Josh!' he called.

'Coming!' shouted Tamsyn.

They all looked towards *GO GAMEZONE*. As Tamsyn clattered down the gangplank, Brad Stewart said loudly to Mr Zanelli, 'Paul, can you lead me to a hot shower?'

'Sure,' said Mr Zanelli.

'While you're doing that, I've got some shopping to do,' said Mrs Zanelli. She turned to Rob. 'Are you coming?'

'Is it all right if we stay here and look around?' said Rob. 'Tamsyn will make sure I don't fall in!'

Mrs Zanelli smiled and nodded. As she walked off in one direction, Brad Stewart and Mr Zanelli walked off the opposite way.

Rob took a deep breath. 'OK. Here goes. The big sting. Ready?'

Tamsyn pulled out Mitch's copy of the Turner.

It was no longer in its padded envelope, but simply wrapped in brown paper.

'Ready,' said Tamsyn, handing the painting to Rob.

Rob spun round and pushed himself along the quay with Tamsyn following him. As they approached *JIMMY THE ONE*, Gilroy came back up on deck. Rob feigned surprise.

'Hey, Mr Gilroy. Brad's gone off for a shower. He asked me to give you this. "Lucky charm returned," he said.'

Gilroy's face creased in a smile as he took the package. 'Thanks. I was wondering if he'd remember.' The yachtsman dug in his pocket. 'There. Here's his compass. Safe journeys both.'

Without a further word, Gilroy spun on his heel and leapt back onto his yacht.

Tamsyn pushed Rob quickly back down the quay, beyond *GO GAMEZONE*, and round to a corner from where they could keep an eye on both yachts without being spotted.

'Any minute now,' muttered Rob. 'If it's going to work, it's got to happen any minute now.'

'What if he doesn't open it?'

'Tamsyn, you saw his face when he took that parcel. He thinks it's a five million dollar painting. He's *got* to open it straight away! And when he sees it's his copy back again he's—'

'*Got* to come and get the real one,' said Tamsyn, 'while he knows there's nobody on board *GO*—' She didn't finish.

'There he is!' hissed Rob.

Gilroy had reappeared. As they watched from their hiding place, he leapt from the deck of *JIMMY THE ONE*. In his hands was the opened package he'd just taken from Rob. Looking about him, Gilroy moved quickly towards *GO GAMEZONE*.

'He's going on board,' cried Rob. 'It's working! He's going after the real one!'

Hearts pounding, they waited, imagining what was happening – Gilroy, confused and angry at having been given the copy ... taking his chance to check out *GO GAMEZONE* while nobody was on board ... seeing the real Turner painting still in position ... swapping the two ...

'Here he comes!' cried Tamsyn.

Gilroy, a small picture frame clutched to his chest, had emerged from the cockpit of *GO GAMEZONE* ... was looking from side to side again ... had started down the gangplank to the quay ...

It was the moment they were waiting for. As Gilroy left *GO GAMEZONE* and headed for *JIMMY THE ONE*, they dived out from their hiding place.

'Stop him!' screamed Tamsyn.

Gilroy turned, startled. As he saw Tamsyn racing round the corner, with Rob going as quickly as he could behind her, he swung round again and began running ... straight into the solid figures of Brad Stewart and Mrs Zanelli as they jumped out at the other end of the quay.

'No you don't, Gilroy!' yelled Brad, lunging

for Gilroy's arm. 'Forget it!'

Gilroy fought like a demon. Wrenching himself free, he spun round and raced back again, back towards Tamsyn and Rob – and, as he suddenly appeared from behind them, Mr Zanelli.

'There's no way out, Gilroy!' shouted Mr Zanelli. 'Give yourself up.'

Desperately, the cornered man looked for a way to escape. There was nowhere to go. He was surrounded.

'Paul,' shouted Brad Stewart, grabbing Gilroy by both arms, 'get the painting!'

'You'll have to swim for it!' snarled Gilroy … and, before either Mr Zanelli or Brad Stewart could stop him, he'd dropped the painting on the ground and sent it scudding past Tamsyn and towards the edge of the quay.

Rob saw it coming. Unable to keep up with Tamsyn, he'd pushed himself as fast as he could. Now, as the valuable painting skidded along the ground, he changed direction.

His timing was perfect. As he turned, the painting clattered against one of his wheels and stopped.

'Rob!' screamed Tamsyn. 'The water!'

Rob looked up. In changing direction to intercept the Turner he'd sent himself racing towards the edge. He swung round, but the move was too sudden. He felt his wheelchair tipping over, felt himself falling out …

Tamsyn was still a couple of metres away when he began to topple. Launching herself forward, she grabbed hold of the chair's nearest handle and pulled with all her might.

'I can't hold you!' she screamed.

But she'd given Rob the time he needed. As he threw all his weight over to the side Tamsyn was holding, the wheel thudded down onto the solid quayside.

'Rob Zanelli, don't you ever do that to me again!' Tamsyn cried.

Rob grinned. 'I can swim, you know!'

Behind them, Gilroy was struggling in Brad Stewart's vice-like grip.

'You tried to use me, Gilroy,' said Brad angrily. 'And if it hadn't been for these kids, you'd have got away with it.'

Suddenly Gilroy broke free. For a moment he looked as though he was going to run for it again, but then a cool smirk broke across his face.

'You've got nothing on me, Stewart,' he said. '*You* brought that painting across the Atlantic, not me.'

He swung round to face Mr and Mrs Zanelli. 'And that's *your* company's yacht. Not mine.'

Smoothing down his crumpled shirt, Gilroy snarled, 'I'll deny the lot. There's no way you can prove I knew anything about that painting.'

'We can, Mr Gilroy,' said Josh. 'No problem.'

Gilroy's face turned pale. Josh was standing at the cockpit of *GO GAMEZONE*. Held up to his eye, and still running, was the video camera.

'Yeah,' cried Rob and Tamsyn. 'Way to go!'

'I recorded you swapping that copy Rob gave

you for the real one in the saloon, Mr Gilroy. Now why would you do that if you didn't know which painting was which?'

Abbey School. Monday 24th June, 8.55 a.m.

Rob quickly typed the finishing touches to his e-mail. 'OK?' he asked.

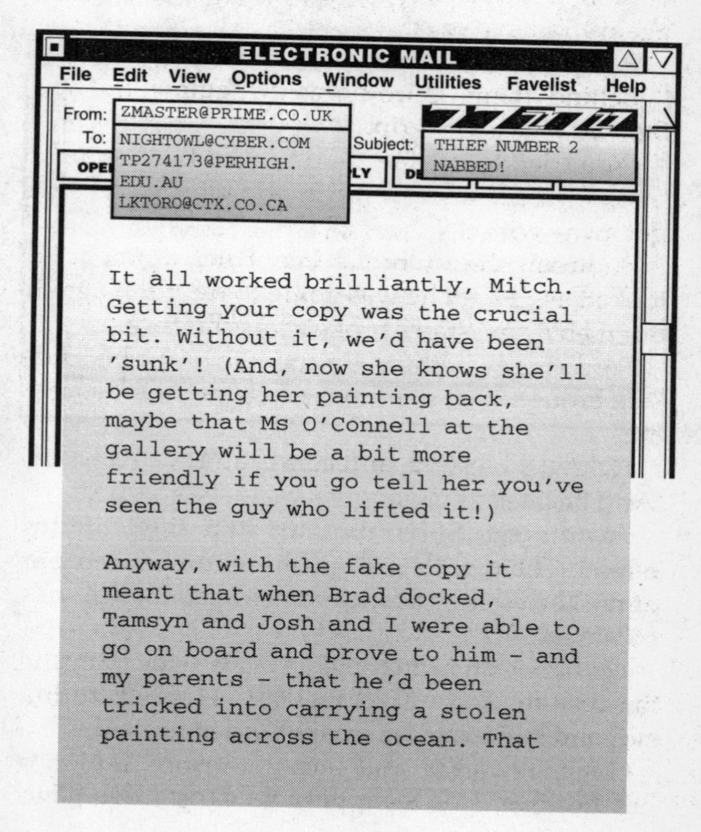

It all worked brilliantly, Mitch. Getting your copy was the crucial bit. Without it, we'd have been 'sunk'! (And, now she knows she'll be getting her painting back, maybe that Ms O'Connell at the gallery will be a bit more friendly if you go tell her you've seen the guy who lifted it!)

Anyway, with the fake copy it meant that when Brad docked, Tamsyn and Josh and I were able to go on board and prove to him - and my parents - that he'd been tricked into carrying a stolen painting across the ocean. That way, they were ready (after *some* persuasion!) to help us with the sting against Gilroy.

Josh hid on GO GAMEZONE (did you know the bench seats in the saloon lift up, like in a caravan?) with the video camera while Tamsyn and I gave Gilroy the copy. All we had to do then was wait for him to realise he'd been done and go on board to try and switch it for the real one – and for Josh to record him doing it!

Funny thing, but when he found out about the video, Gilroy didn't want an action replay for some reason. The police did, though...

Mail:

'OK!' echoed Josh and Tamsyn. 'Now come on, we'll be late!'

Hitting the SEND button, Rob fired off his e-mail. Then, with Josh pushing, they raced out of the Technology Block and across to the school's conference hall.

No sooner had they taken their seats than the familiar figure of Brad Stewart emerged from a side door and strode to the centre of the stage.

'Mr Stewart,' said Mrs Burton, Abbey's headteacher, 'we have been looking forward to

your visit immensely. Rob has told us all so much about you. And … well … all I can do is hand over to you. I'm sure you've got a wonderful tale to tell.'

Brad smiled and stepped forward. 'Thank you, Mrs Burton. And when I've finished …' he scanned the audience until he spotted the faces he was looking for, '… maybe we can persuade Rob, Tamsyn and Josh over there to do some talking. Because they've got an even *better* tale to tell!'

INTERNET DETECTIVES

michael coleman

NET BANDITS

TAMSYN, GET HELP
: - ((¬: - D : - Vi-)

A new message suddenly appears on Tamsyn's computer screen from the mystery kid who calls himself ZMASTER. Is it a joke, or is he in real trouble? Tamsyn and Josh are sure something is seriously wrong. But how can they help him when they don't know who he is?
Electronic messages flash round the globe as friends thousands of miles apart try to find a boy in terrible danger . . .

But will the Internet reveal its secrets in time?

Other books in the series ▷

michael coleman

ESCAPE KEY

The man's face stared out at them from the computer screen.

'It is him!' exclaimed Rob.

The photograph, flashed instantly from Australia via the Internet, sets Rob, Tamsyn and Josh on a thrilling hunt for a man wanted by the police on two continents.

They've seen him once already, but they've no idea where he is now. With the help of brilliant detective work by their friends on the Net, they start to track down their mysterious subject . . .

Other books in the series ▷

michael coleman

CYBER FEUD

Tamsyn pointed at the screen. 'The system says you logged in yesterday.'

'But I didn't!' cried Josh. 'You've got to believe me!'

Years before, Josh Allen's father was blamed for a crime he didn't commit. Can Josh, Tamsyn and Rob use their contacts on the Net to prove Mr Allen's innocence after all these years?

The trail leads them round the world – but only to discover that somebody else is always one step ahead of them. Then Josh himself is accused of a crime. He swears he's innocent. Who is making history repeat itself? And why?

Publication October 1996

Other books in the series ▷

INTERNET DETECTIVES